THE AMISH COWBOY

Large Print edition

Montana Millers
Book 1

ADINA SENFT

Moonshell
Books

Cover design by Carpe Librum Book Design. Images used under license.

German quotations from the 1912 Luther Bible, with English from the King James Version.

The Amish Cowboy / Adina Senft—1st ed large print

ISBN 978-1-950854-52-3 R070222

❀ Created with Vellum

Praise for Adina Senft

"Filled with spiritual insights and multilayered storylines. At times readers will be chuckling and other times, misty eyed as the book unfolds."

Amish Reader on *Herb of Grace*

"A heart-warming tale that celebrates the best things about being Amish."

Christian Fiction Addiction on *Keys of Heaven*

"Adina Senft has once again produced a simply sweet and engaging Amish romance novel, filled with twists and turns, enjoyable beyond compare."

Amish Reader on *Balm of Gilead*

In this series
AMISH COWBOYS

The Montana Millers

The Amish Cowboy
The Amish Cowboy's Baby
The Amish Cowboy's Bride
The Amish Cowboy's Letter
The Amish Cowboy's Makeover
The Amish Cowboy's Home

Acknowledgments

Grateful thanks to ranchers Einar and Judy Nelson and to Captain Brent Kirk, rancher, firefighter and all-around hero. Your help has been invaluable in bringing the Circle M to life. Thanks also to Heather J. Graham for facilitating conversations, to Nancy Warren and Jennifer Skully for their encouragement and support, and to Jeff, for once again being willing to pack up the pickup and head off on the next research trip.

THE AMISH COWBOY

Chapter 1
MOUNTAIN HOME, MONTANA

"GOD IS GOOD, and northwestern Montana is the proof."

Daniel Miller laid a hand on his mare's neck as she sidestepped, and gazed out at the forests and meadows of the high country, with Siksika Lake set like a jewel in the cupped hands of the mountains. They had brought the horses to a halt on a knoll that Daniel knew was one of Dat's favorite places to give thanks, as he was doing now. Above them, a hawk balanced on the updraft created by the looming bulk of the mountain, and off to the left, deer grazed on one side of a grassy clearing.

Behind them in the acres of the collection field, cattle milled and lowed, the females looking to mother up with their calves, calves bawling as they tried to find the mothers they'd been separated from when the cowboys had brought them down from the forests and meadows of the high country over the past week.

Daniel's father, Reuben, pushed up the brim of his black winter work hat with one gloved finger. "We have a lot to be thankful for. That the *gut Gott* made this country. That He led me here when my brothers were determined that I follow them to Colorado and New Mexico. And that He gave me and your *mamm* a fine family to help us care for it."

"I'll agree with you on all but the last one. I think the *gut Gott* might have been distracted when it came to making the twins."

Reuben laughed. "I must say that those girls are a handful—worse than you four boys together. But they seemed to have settled some now. Rebecca plans to start baptism classes and join church in the spring, she tells me."

"Does she?" Daniel's heart swelled, and the sun seemed to lie with greater warmth on his shoulders. "Let's hope Malena takes her good example to heart."

"She is in God's hands, *mei Sohn*, and there is no safer place."

Reuben gathered up his gelding's reins and they rode down the path single file, the horses sensing instinctively that today's inspection of the cattle was over, and it was time to go home. In Amish communities in other states, the elders frowned on riding horses, which were meant to pull buggies and to work in the fields. But Amish communities in other states didn't sprawl across mountains with steep sides and narrow trails. If a rancher did not hold with gas-powered quad-runners—noisy, smelly things that only frightened the cattle—then using a horse for riding was certainly the lesser of two evils. So, the Circle M kept cutting horses for ranch work, and buggy horses for transportation.

Daniel patted Marigold's neck again in appreciation. The twins had named the cutting horses after flowers, regardless of what their actual names had been at the time, and Dat had laughed and gone along with it. Daniel supposed he should be thankful they'd stopped before they got to Skunk Cabbage or Hydrangea.

He gazed up at the ranks of the Rockies marching into the distance, their jagged peaks white with new snow. "So, Dat, we start trailing them down day after tomorrow? Rafe Williams at the Bar Z has already taken his, and I expect John Mackenzie will follow soon."

His father nodded. The trails were already trampled from the movement of their neighbors' herds. "*Ja*, it's time. The Bar Z and the Star are bigger outfits than we are, so it's right they started early. Our neighbors and some in the church are just waiting for us to give the word. The weather isn't supposed to change until next week, but it's October. You know how that goes."

Montana weather was notoriously unpredictable, and even though the last week of September had been warm, since then there had been a skiff of snow down in the home paddocks. Daniel was grateful for their neighbors, both *Englisch* and Amish, who considered roundup a community event. All the neighboring ranches ran their cattle on the surrounding allotments. They weren't fenced, so the animals could get to the grazing land, and the animals often wandered on to the Bureau of Land Management land as well. Sorting one ranch's cattle from another took place in the collection fields, where it was manageable, and now his family were ready for the final stage of the process: trailing their own cattle down to the Circle M seven miles away.

The steep trail widened out as they reached

the open country. Daniel inspected the way, looking for washouts or mud holes that might snag an unsuspecting calf or cause a neighbor's horse to throw an inexperienced rider or injure itself. But with the herds coming down so recently, the wide track was plain and unobstructed. At the gate that gave on to the county road, Daniel allowed his father to ride through first, then closed and secured the gate behind them both.

The law of the gate, he had learned even before he was old enough to reach the latch, meant that you left it as you found it. Always. No exceptions.

After four miles along the road, the horses broke into a trot when they saw the familiar fences and fields of home in the distance. His own half-constructed house lay just visible to the west, its roof and walls newly dried in and waiting for the many hours of elbow grease he'd put in during the short days and long evenings of winter. The sight always gave Daniel a pang of happiness at homecoming, with a soft edge of longing. Longing for a wife, a partner who would share the joys and burdens of life with him, doubling the one and halving the other. For children they might bring up in the fear of the Lord, teaching them the Amish ways that had been handed down for hundreds of years.

Unbidden, her face flashed into his memory—those gray eyes, the pain in them as she told him she could not marry him. Lovina Wengerd Lapp had stayed in Whinburg Township where it was safe, and married someone else. Not a cowboy whose life on the ranch could sometimes be as difficult as it was rewarding, but a baker or a harness maker or something. A man who stayed inside to make his living.

Daniel shook away the unkind memories and allowed the beauty of the country to soak into his soul. His parents' ranch house stood on a slight rise farther up the valley, facing south, to gather in as much light and warmth as possible during short winter days. Daadi Miller, and the teenage Reuben with his two brothers Marlon and David, had built it in the seventies when their family had settled here, an easy buggy ride to the town of Mountain Home. More and more families had come to settle, and now the *Englisch* tourists were coming to enjoy the homemade goods at the bakery, the variety in the general store, the handcrafted ironwork and quilts. Their own log house with its peaked roof jutting out over the front deck seemed to welcome visitors, and on church Sundays the front room held all the *Gmee*, with the view through the windows of the land God had created, to remind them of all they had to be grateful for.

The bunkhouse and cattle barns, and his own house as well, were constructed using the same methods, out of sturdy logs with corrugated metal roofs that would let snow slide harmlessly away. Even the chicken house fit the pattern, large enough for the fifty birds and the few speckled guinea hens that were cared for by Mamm and the twins.

After unsaddling the horses, currying them, and putting them in their stalls with the feed they'd been hoping for, Reuben told him, "I'll make those calls. No sense wasting time."

Other Amish communities might have a telephone hanging in the barn, or in a phone shanty out on the road. But here in Montana, life was a little more challenging than in the older, more established communities in Indiana and Pennsylvania and Ohio. Between high country and weather, and the distance between families, it had become clear to the elders both here and in Colorado that cell phones were necessary for safety. There was even a cell tower on the Stolzfus place that brought a little extra income from the phone company to the widow Rose.

So while Dat leaned on a post in the barn to make his calls, watching the horses enjoy their oats, Daniel walked up to the house.

"You're back!" Malena met him at the door and then hollered over her shoulder, "Mamm, Daniel and Dat are back."

"Don't sound so surprised." He grinned at his sister, who was twenty-two, but whose merry eyes and small figure made her look still in her teens. Her prayer covering was neatly pinned on curly brown hair that never stayed quite as neat as Rebecca's straighter hair seemed to, a fact that caused significant aggravation every church Sunday.

"I'm not surprised. I'm glad." Malena hugged him, a brief, fierce hug that nearly squeezed the breath out of him. "When is roundup?"

"Day after tomorrow."

She whooped and grabbed a barn coat off the hook. "I'll tell the boys."

"Dat is out there, he will—"

But she was already out the door, and here came Rebecca down the stairs from their room. "Tomorrow? Goodness, I've got to get Lilac ready then, and clean her tack, and—"

Another barn jacket vanished and the door slammed behind her.

"And they say there are no tornadoes in Montana," he said into the silence. Daniel heard a quiet chuckle and turned to see his mother in the kitchen doorway, wiping her hands on a dish towel.

Naomi Miller smiled a welcome, and tilted her head toward the kitchen. "Gingerbread whoopie pies cooling on the counter. One thing about your sisters—any job they tackle gets done in a hurry."

"Even if you have to make them do it over again?" He took a whoopie pie and the warm scent of ginger and cream-cheese frosting filled his nose as he bit into it.

"Not so much anymore. Even Malena learned eventually that if you do something properly the first time, you have more time afterward to do your own things. Simple arithmetic. And at least they got the pies done. I only have to frost the rest and put them together."

"These are good." Daniel took another. "Dat's in the barn making the calls. Day after tomorrow."

Mamm nodded. "We'll give everyone breakfast, as usual. We've got elk sausage, bacon and mushroom casserole, and a couple of pigs' weight in pork sausage. That should hold you all until lunch."

"You and the girls are riding out, too?"

"The girls wouldn't miss this. But I'll stay here with the women who aren't riding." She brushed a bit of frosting from the stubble on his cheek. "You need a shave if you're going to catch a girl's eye, *mei Sohn*."

"Hey, I've been chasing cattle for two days," he defended himself. As if she couldn't tell by the smell of horse and the stains on his jeans. "Besides, all the girls in this neck of the woods have their eyes on someone else. I've got used to being the third oldest bachelor in the district."

"Third? Who might the first two be?" She was trying not to smile, and failing completely.

"Josiah and John Bontrager."

His mother's laughter always delighted Daniel. It sounded like a rushing creek and birdsong and kindness, if that were possible. "Those old bachelors! They've got forty years on you and even yet, I know a widow or two who would light a candle in the window if she thought one would come calling."

Now it was his turn to laugh. "I'm barely twenty-eight, Mamm. When God sends me the woman He means for me, I'll be ready and waiting."

His mother had crossed the kitchen and bent to open the propane oven's door, which was why he thought she said, "He already did."

But that couldn't be right. Mamm had never met Lovina Lapp.

Daniel snagged a third whoopie pie on his way out the door. He had chores waiting, and an hour yet until supper.

Chapter 2

TWO DAYS LATER, the entire Miller family was up and at work by four a.m. While the twins helped Mamm in the kitchen, preparing an enormous breakfast for twenty people, Daniel and his brothers went down to the barn to get the horses tacked up and ready. Well, Zach and Adam were helping. Joshua, who at twenty-one was the youngest of his brothers, had a gift for finding something to do that wasn't the task at hand, and managed to skate out from under the work his brothers did.

Not today. Daniel set him to preparing trail bundles.

"What for?" Joshua wanted to know. "It's not

like we're going to be camping up there like last week. We'll be back by nightfall."

"Never hurts to be prepared." Daniel handed him a stack of waterproof stuff bags. "There could be a freak blizzard, like the one four years ago. What would have happened to you then if we hadn't had tents and camping mats?"

"I'd be dead, probably. Frozen solid until spring." That was one thing about Josh. Daniel could usually get him to see reason. Once he saw it, he was more happy to do what was asked of him. But if he couldn't see the reason for something, he was as slippery as a calf in a mudhole and usually went scrambling off in another direction.

"Besides, the horses carry the extra," Adam pointed out, invisible behind a stall wall, where he was checking his horse's feet. "Not like anyone is asking you to pack it all in on your back."

"Everyone carries their own lunches. No chuck wagon this year?" Zach pushed his glasses up with a gesture similar to the one Dat used to adjust his hat. At twenty-six, Zach was the next in age to Daniel. It was comical how much he was like their father in body, and how far apart they were in other ways. While Dat loved the land and the animals it nurtured, Zach was interested in the homes people lived in. He'd been nagging the folks over at Meadowlark to take him on as a member of their crew so he could learn the ins and outs of building log houses, but hadn't succeeded yet. Now, at the end of the building season, he'd have to wait until spring. Maybe that was God's will, too, along with finding a partner in life.

"*Neh*, we're leaving the chuck wagon home." Daniel lifted down the camping mats and the pup tents. Two people fit comfortably in a tent. He'd spent more than one night in the meadows of the high country in the spring, talking over life with Adam, his middle brother, or Zach, in the shelter of one of these tents. They weren't meant for long-term camping. They were just in case of the unexpected. "Best go find the backpacks. I think they're in the office closet."

Zach returned a few minutes later. "I'll run these up to Mamm so the girls can fill them after breakfast."

Some ranchers' allotments were farther away than a day's ride, so they'd use a chuck wagon. Not like the old relics Daniel had seen in history books. Rather, it was an enclosed vehicle that had been an Amish buggy in a former life, now fitted out with a camp stove, propane tank, and storage for food and pans. It lived at Bishop Wengerd's place and was rolled out whenever it was needed.

There was that pang in his heart again. Daniel shook his head at himself as he heaved a saddle on to Marigold's blanketed back. Wengerd had been Lovina's maiden name. The two families were related, but "Little Joe" Wengerd, the six-foot-five head of the Montana branch of the family and their community's bishop, hadn't been back to Whinburg Township in thirty years. Some thought it was because he'd had a falling-out with his brother, Lovina's grandfather. Others that he disliked travel by train. But Little Joe had once told Daniel that it was because of the cattle.

"Hard to leave 'em," he'd said. "Can't just go away for a month in any season. The Lord has made me responsible for 'em, as well as for the church, so I've got to be a good husbandman to both and stay where He's put me."

Bless Little Joe, who pressed into the center of God's will. It was pointless to think about Lovina. Worse than pointless—it was a little too close to complaining about that same will. God's will was perfect, and Lovina was living within it. What Daniel needed to do was draw closer, too, like

Little Joe. Only there would he find the peace he craved.

———

BY SIX A.M. THE sky glowed, telling them sunrise wasn't far away and making the quaking aspens turn molten gold with reflected light. Mist rose from the home fields, where the fences looked like ghosts, the white vapor eddying with the movement of the buggy horses, who would not be going along. Joshua and a couple of the younger teenage boys ran hither and yon, doing last-minute tasks that no one had asked for, while *Englisch* and Amish neighbors came riding or driving up the gravel lane in twos and threes.

Daniel felt as though he ought to be mounted up, riding the edge of the milling crowd to keep them all together, the way he did the cattle before Dat whistled and headed out. Instead, he was trying not to look at his sisters' getups—they wore jeans and boots under their modest dresses so that they could ride astride. Both girls had tied scarves over their braided buns, with shapeless hats on top to keep off the sun later, and keep their heads warm now. The air was frigid, frost riming the roofs of the buildings and edging every vein in the fallen leaves. They all had their winter coats on, and Daniel was thankful his horse would help keep his legs warm until the sun was properly up.

Here came the Wengerd party, the bishop with his snow-white beard leading the way. He'd already brought his animals down to his own ranch with the Millers' help. It would never occur to him not to return the favor. Among the buggies was one driven by his wife, Sadie, accompanied by her youngest daughter Ruby and what looked like another woman. Another buggy was driven by one of her daughters-in-law and brought Sadie's grandchildren, while her two grown sons rode. And what was this? Who belonged to the little boy riding an old horse so stiffly in front of Little Joe's eldest son? Neither of the sons had a boy big enough to—

The buggies rolled to a stop and the occupants spilled out.

"Mamm! Mamm, did you see? Cousin Peter let me ride the whole way all by myself!"

A laughing woman looked up at the excited boy and laid a hand on his leg. "You did so well, and the horse obeyed you."

"He's a natural," Peter Wengerd said, leaning

on his saddle horn while Daniel's heart came to a complete halt in his chest.

As though a gong had rung to get her attention, the boy's mother turned, and for the second time in his life, Daniel Miller was poleaxed by a pair of gray eyes, starred with long lashes that had once given him "butterfly kisses" all over his face. Those graceful hands had once cupped his jaw. That rose-petal mouth had once said things to make a man's heart burn with hope … and in the end said words that had simply burned.

Lovina-love.

Her face had gone white as frost, and yet she did not look away.

"Daniel!" Adam and Zach flanked him. "Daniel? Hey!" Adam squeezed his arm. "*Was ischt?*"

All at once the sounds of horses stamping, neighbors talking, and harness jingling flooded into his ears. His feet in their sturdy Western boots were firmly on the ground, and he was no longer floating in some cloudlike place where only the two of them existed.

"What?" he said.

"Little Joe says some of their company might want to come along. They only got here yesterday."

They'd arrived yesterday? Had she been here a whole day and he had not known?

Don't be an idiot, he told himself. There's no connection between you anymore. She is married and clearly that is her child and there's an end of it. Her husband was probably one of the riders still coming in, or maybe he was driving a buggy.

And now here they came, to greet Dat and Mamm. When she had spoken to them and given them the Whinburg connections' greetings, she turned to him.

"Daniel," she said.

His heart did a kind of belly-flop in his chest at the sound of his name in that musical voice. "Lovina. Welcome to the Circle M. Is that your boy?"

For answer, she turned. "Joel! *Kumm hier.*"

The boy ran up obediently. Here were Lovina's gray eyes under a mop of chocolate-brown hair. That must come from her husband, because her hair was as fair and shining as a skein of silk.

"Joel, this is Daniel Miller, Reuben's oldest son."

The boy ducked his head. "*Guder mariye,* Daniel. *Denki* for letting us come today."

He wasn't aware that he had. "I'm glad you

could. But how—" *How did you come to be here at all?*

"It's a long story," she said, "but the short version is that we joined a party of people who hired an *Englisch* van for a touring holiday."

"We've seen eight national parks out of twelve," Joel said eagerly. "At Yellowstone we saw the geyser. And at Glacier there was a big bear and a herd of elk and—" He stopped. "And then the van died."

"So I borrowed someone's phone to call Cousin Joe and he told us the Amtrak stops at Libby. We have to make arrangements to travel home." A flush burned into her face. "I had no idea that we would be interrupting the ranch work in this way."

"You aren't interrupting," Little Joe rumbled, coming up behind her in time to hear. "It'll be good for you to get up into God's country."

"But we're not going," she protested. "I said I would help with the cooking."

Little Joe looked down at her, compassion written in his face. "You need a change, cousin. Take your mind off—everything."

"He means my *dat*," Joel supplied somberly, looking up at Daniel. "The national parks were supposed to do that, but even when I saw the geyser, all I could think was how he would have liked it."

Lovina bent to hug him. "Of course you think of him, and you should. He was a good man who deserves our good memories. But *der Herr* decided that it was Dat's time, and so we must accept His will."

He *would have* liked it? *Dat's time?* Did that mean—

Daniel's heart did a swan dive off a high precipice.

Lovina Lapp was a widow?

Chapter 3

LOVINA STRAIGHTENED, doing her best to sound calm when all she wanted to do was take Joel by the hand and run away down the gravel lane. "We will stay here at the house and help with the work."

"But Maaaammmm," Joel wailed.

Cousin Joe clearly knew children, even bereaved eight-year-olds who had never seen so many changes in so short a time. *"Kumm mit,"* he said, offering Joel his hand. "Let's eat a good breakfast and then we'll see."

Hmph. There was nothing to see.

Her back was to Daniel, and the fact that her skin was prickling under his gaze as though he had touched her was simply her imagination.

Nothing to see there either. Only the shock in his face that no doubt had mirrored her own. She had known there was a branch of the Whinburg Township Millers here, of course, and Melvin and Carrie Miller in Willow Creek had given her messages to pass on if their paths crossed. But she'd never thought their paths actually would— Montana had not even been on the Troyers' itinerary when she'd accepted their kind invitation.

As the crowd walked up to the house, she eyed Daniel covertly. She hadn't seen him since that last horrible conversation nine years ago, when they'd both been too young for him to ask the question he should never have asked. He had changed. Become a man, with broad, capable shoulders under his black coat, and a stride that spoke of comfort with himself and with the land, of a certain authority. She had seen hints of it back then, but now it had come to fruition. Oh, Reuben Miller was definitely in charge, but it was clear that Daniel was his right hand. The prosperity of the ranch was the result of many years of the family's labor, she could see that.

This was where he belonged.

And where she did not.

She was being schooled in patience, though Cousin Joe Wengerd, the community's bishop, did not know it. With every fiber of her being, she wanted to get on the train and go back to Whinburg Township, but she and the Troyer party had to wait until roundup was concluded before Joe would have the time to help. She must submit, and do her best to keep Joel safe from trampling hooves and bears and goodness knew what other dangers this wild country harbored for the unwary.

Yesterday Cousin Joe had suggested they have a couple of riding lessons, so to please him, she and Joel had listened carefully as Ruby showed them how reins were handled on a cutting horse as opposed to a buggy horse, how to use their feet in the stirrups, the uncomfortable difference between a trot and a canter, and how to saddle and unsaddle the animal. Joel had loved it. Lovina was still sore. As she ate her share of the huge breakfast and had a second cup of the best coffee she'd tasted so far on this trip, she made up her mind that, instead of giving in to Cousin Joe, she would stick with her decision to stay behind with the women and lend a hand here.

Daniel would ride away and be gone the whole day, and when the day was over, she and Joel would go back to the Bar Z. And that would be that.

It was clear that on his side at least, bygones were bygones, which was just as it should be. Mose had only been gone eleven months, so it was not fitting for her to be so aware of Daniel, so conscious that he was quite content to talk and laugh with those sitting closer than she was, including a girl called Susan Bontrager, who sat with his sisters as though they were in the same buddy bunch. What did she expect? Lovina was just someone from his past with whom he'd shared a magical summer—and everyone knew that summer love was as fleeting as a firefly's spark. What she'd had with Mose was winter love —born of long conversations in his parents' kitchen as the snow flew, long days in the antique shop as he'd labored extra hours to save enough money for them to be married. Winter love knew waiting and endurance, not ease and laughter. They'd moved into the tiny apartment over the antique shop, and when Joel had been born the following autumn, her first winter as a mother had been a joy.

And if sometimes she longed for summer? Well, that was just her earthly nature, and she did her best to stifle it. She had made the right choice. The safe choice. And Joel had grown up healthy and happy, bright and curious, reminding her more every day that while the night had been long, joy came in the morning. She was solely responsible for him now, and it was her job to keep him safe.

It was not until she got up to help clear the table that her sensible plans went off the rails.

"*Neh*, Lovina," Naomi Miller said, putting an arm around her shoulders and steering her toward the stairs. "You don't have time if you're going to go with them. I know you don't have work clothes along, but I can lend you some of mine. Your own boots will be fine for the day."

"But I'm not going with them." She was acutely aware that even in the chaos of leaving the big dining room, people were glancing their way. "Joel and I are staying here."

"I thought Little Joe's Ruby gave you riding lessons yesterday?" Naomi's blue eyes were puzzled.

"She did," Lovina said with a smile. "And today my sore legs are telling me I'd better stay behind."

"Riding will work the soreness out of—"

Joel broke free of two *Englisch* boys who had come in one of the neighbors' parties. From their clothes, it was clear they were going up the mountain, too. "Mamm, Evan and Jack say they'll teach me how to rope. Please can we go?"

"Joel, I said no."

His face crumpled and despite the satisfying breakfast, tears welled in his eyes. Bravely, he tried to blink them back.

"What's this?" Cousin Joe said. "Not go? Joel did well yesterday. It would be a shame to leave him behind. He can ride with Adam and Zach if you don't want him going with the Martin boys. He'll come to no harm."

"I don't—" Lovina began.

"I know how you feel," Naomi said. "But think what a good experience this will be for Joel. He'll have all the men around him, and my boys will look out for him."

"It's only up and back. Eight years is plenty old enough to be without you for a day," Little Joe said gruffly.

In her son's eyes she could see the conflict. He wanted to go. At the same time, he was afraid to go alone. He would never say it in front of the men, but she knew her boy. New experiences— like riding a horse instead of driving it—were scary. That's why she had taken lessons with him yesterday, too. Little did she know she'd been creating expectations in the Wengerds that she hadn't meant to fulfill.

The chaos increased as people pulled on coats

and hats, and she even heard the jingle of spurs on the boots of a few of the *Englisch* men. And in the midst of it stood Daniel with that look on his face she remembered so acutely. Compassion. And pity. Pity that she was so timid. The same look he had worn when she'd given him her answer and told him why.

How dared he look at her that way when she'd been through childbirth and her husband's death —two things he had never experienced!

His sisters and Susan Bontrager surrounded him with a sudden barrage of questions, and the look vanished as he turned to answer them. But that moment had been enough.

If they wanted Joel to go, then she would, too. After all, as Little Joe said, it was only for a day. She could do anything for a day.

"Very well," she said. "Naomi, if you can lend me some things, I can be ready in five minutes."

———

BY THE THIRD mile along the county road, the sun had come up and Lovina was regretting that moment of stung pride. And by the time they had passed through a cattle gate and begun a gentle climb up through the grassy meadowlands, all she could think about was the need to stay on this horse and endure. Her heart-shaped Lancaster County *Kapp* had been left behind and her hair bound up in a navy blue *Duchly*. She wore one of the Miller brothers' hats instead of her own away bonnet, and a pair of someone's twenty-year-old blue jeans under her black dress to protect her legs and her modesty. On her back was a small rucksack stuffed with her and Joel's lunch, and behind her saddle was a "trail bundle" that held things she devoutly hoped she'd never have to use.

Naomi had sent her off on a mare named Rosie. "She's an experienced cattle horse, but she's gentle," Naomi had said when Lovina had mounted up. "Just don't let her take off after a runaway calf. She'll want to, because that's her job, but she'll obey you."

Lovina had smiled and tried to look confident. "*Denki*, Naomi. See you tonight."

She didn't have to worry about keeping up— Rosie knew her business. And when the horse broke into a trot on the wide, grassy track along with the others, she barely had time to make a muffled exclamation before Malena and Susan had flanked her. "Go with her motion," Malena advised. "Don't be afraid to lift up and down if you have to, or slow her. Remember, the two of you are a team."

"She and your *mamm* are a team," Lovina corrected the girl breathlessly. "I'm just baggage, like the trail bundle."

The girls laughed as though she'd made a joke. Ahead, Joel rode between Adam and Zachariah, looking far more comfortable already than he had been yesterday during their lessons. He had always liked working with the horses with his father, driving the spring wagon from one place to another in search of antiques for the shop. Maybe he was what the *Englisch* called "a natural." She saw how he lifted up and down in rhythm with the horse's feet, and did her best to mimic it. At least her spine wouldn't be pounded quite as flat this way.

Somehow Susan Bontrager got separated from their group of young women, and the quartet became a trio, then a duet. The next time Lovina looked, the girl was riding next to Daniel as the trail narrowed and climbed between the pines.

Malena giggled. "There she goes."

"Who?" Lovina asked her.

"Susan. My brother is so clueless." She rolled

her eyes. "I told her she'd have to be as forward as she knows how if she wants to get his attention."

With as much nonchalance as she could muster, Lovina said, "And does she want it?"

"Oh, *ja*. Susan's been crazy about him for ages. But it's like he has a blind spot where girls are concerned. She's not the first to try, but I hope she's the last. I'd love her for a sister-in-law."

"Doesn't he want to get married? Twenty-eight is leaving it a bit late."

Malena shot a curious look at her. "Good guess."

She'd slipped up, revealing that she knew his age. Clearly Daniel had never told his family what had happened the summer he'd gone east. "I met your brother years ago, in Whinburg Township."

"That summer he went out to work? We must have been what, twelve maybe? Because we built the new barn the summer after, and I remember our relatives in Willow Creek invited him, but he didn't go because Dat needed him." She rode for a few yards, looking thoughtful. "I suppose he does want to get married. He joined church that spring, before the barn went up, so there's nothing stopping him. But there aren't that many prospects around here. Susan and maybe two or

three others. There are more families in St. Ignatius, but it's a long way to go for a date."

"He could move somewhere else," Lovina suggested, though she already knew what his sister
would say.

Malena laughed. "Not Daniel. He's as rooted
here as—as one of those pines." She waved at the
ranks of trees marching up the hill on their right.
"He's already building his house in the meadow
down the valley. It'll be done by spring." She
twinkled at Lovina. "It wouldn't surprise me if
Susan hasn't already decided how the house will
be finished and what the paint colors will be.
She's a planner, that one. Likes to be prepared."

Was she, now. Well, Lovina wished her well in
her pursuit. Because only a woman who already
lived here could be prepared for the wildness of
Montana. What must it be like in the winter? It
was cold enough in Pennsylvania, but you had
neighbors all around you to help if something
went wrong. What kinds of disasters did the
people here have to deal with?

Now the trail narrowed even further, and the
horses strung out into a long line, single file.
Lovina looked anxiously for Joel, and found him
sandwiched between Rebecca in front and Daniel
behind, somehow managing to chatter with them

both at once. Susan, she was interested to note, had fallen back a couple of places. Rosie seemed to feel the reins go slack, for she looked up at Lovina as if to say, *Pay attention.* Obediently, Lovina gathered them in her gloved hands and allowed herself to breathe the pine-scented air. It was invigorating. And with the horses at a walk, she found herself almost enjoying it.

Almost.

Chapter 4

IT TOOK everything Daniel had to keep his mind on the entire party, and not spend the ride beside Lovina, encouraging her and trying to make her comfortable in a situation where she clearly was not. He had to admit, though, that she was holding her own without his help. At least she was familiar enough with horses that she hadn't fallen off—not that Rosie would have allowed that. Lovina had told him years ago that she and her girlfriends used to ride bareback when they were out in the pasture out of sight of the house, so it wasn't as though she was a complete novice. But there was a big difference between a grassy pasture full of wildflowers and a steep hillside bristling with pines, and dry grass that no longer held any nutrition for the cattle.

There was only one thing he could do for her, and that was to watch after her boy. Thankfully, Susan Bontrager had stopped talking about who would be driving whom after the singing on Friday night, and fallen back in the line. He was too old for the singings now, and hadn't even done much of a *Rumspringe* before he'd joined church. Not like Joshua, who was making a career out of his running-around season. More often than not, there was something on the ranch that demanded Daniel's attention, and he'd rather do that.

Rebecca, seeing that her twin was riding close to Lovina, had instinctively led off with Joel. Dat probably expected him up front, but Adam had already moved into that place. Behind them, Little Joe's two grown sons spaced themselves among the inexperienced Troyers. Following the *Englisch* riders from the neighboring ranches, Little Joe himself brought up the rear. An un-spoken decision had been made even among the *Englisch* to look after the visitors from Pennsylvania, all of whom had never ridden a trail in their lives.

"What kind of bird is that?" Joel asked now, pointing.

"That's a red-tailed hawk," Daniel told him. "See how his wings aren't moving? He's riding the updraft that's coming up the side of the mountain to save his energy while he looks for prey."

"Because hot air rises," the boy said, nodding.

He was a smart one. From being scared and silent, he'd opened up once they'd left the road, and everything he saw interested him.

"Hear that squawking in the pines?" Daniel said. "That's a Steller's jay, warning his family about the hawk. Birds have one call for alarms, another to talk to their family, and sometimes they just sing because *Gott* made them so."

"There's a squirrel! He's so fat."

Daniel smiled. "Close. That's a woodchuck. How much wood can a woodchuck chuck if a woodchuck could chuck wood?"

Joel laughed with delight and repeated the tongue twister. Out of the corner of his eye, Daniel saw Lovina come to attention at his laugh and then smile as she relaxed.

Rebecca taught Joel Peter Piper and his pickled peppers, and then the boy taught her the one about seashells by the seashore, and soon they were gabbling like a pair of geese as one raced to finish a twister before the other.

The seven miles up to the allotment had never gone so quickly. Between enjoying Joel's interest in his surroundings and the occasional surreptitious glance at the boy's mother, plus keeping a watchful eye on the other members of the party, for Daniel the time fled away. It was close to noon when they rode through the gate and trotted into the collection field, where a couple hundred head of cattle were milling.

"How did they all get here?" Joel asked in amazement as Lovina rode up beside him.

"Everything all right, Joel?" she asked.

"*Ja, Mamm*. I had fun with Daniel and Rebecca." He looked up at Daniel. "Do the cows all know to come?"

Daniel moved Marigold slightly to include Lovina. "Some of them do. Those animals will lead the way back, too, probably. But we've been roaming the mountains for the last week or so, bringing them down in small groups. So now, we have to cut out the pairs."

"That sounds painful," Lovina said.

He shook his head. "It just means we divide the herd. Make sure the mothers and calves go together. We don't want anybody getting separated."

"Why not?" Joel wanted to know. "They look old enough. They're not babies anymore."

"They haven't been weaned yet?" Lovina asked Daniel.

"*Neh.* We'll do that in the home pastures, before the trucks come to take them to market."

"What happens if they do get separated?" Joel asked. "Do they cry?"

"*Ja,* but that's not the trouble. Think what would happen if we trailed the herd halfway down, and then a calf decides he's going to go find his mother. He doesn't look in the herd around him. He goes to find her in the last place he nursed."

"Oh-oh," Lovina said. "That could be way up the mountain." Mother and son took in the vastness of the mountainsides as they lifted toward heaven, their peaks already white with snow.

"And then you have to go find them again?" the boy asked incredulously. "Up there?"

"We do." Daniel nodded. "Every one."

"But how do you know you have them all?" Lovina shook her head at the enormity of such a job.

He grinned. "We counted them in May, before we brought them up."

She laughed and rolled her eyes at herself. "Of course you did. What a silly question."

"It wasn't silly, Mamm," Joel told her. "I wondered the same thing."

Reuben Miller whistled, three short, sharp blasts, and Daniel's brothers and the Wengerd boys spurred their horses into motion. "Time to go to work," Daniel said, settling his hat firmly on his head.

"Cutting out pairs," Joel said, as though fixing the term in his memory.

"Yep." Marigold was already straining at the bit, so he let her go and plunged into the melee.

———

LOVINA HAD NEVER SEEN anything like it. Never knew that a horse and rider could move as one being, the horses trained to respond to the slightest pressure of knee and heel. How many years did it take to develop that kind of skill? Daniel and his brothers separated animals out of a herd of their fellows as easily as she separated eggs when she was baking.

"How do they do it?" she asked no one in particular, shaking her head slowly in amazement. Rosie moved restlessly, as though she felt she ought to be working, not standing under the trees watching.

"They are skilled." Susan rode up in time to hear. "But you should see the rodeo cowboys in competition. That is something else." Behind her, Rebecca and Malena were helping Little Joe and the *Englisch* boys keep the non-maternal animals in a separate group. "Those older ones will go down first," Susan went on. "That way, if we have any runaways, they won't spook the entire herd following and the men will have half a chance of catching them."

"Have you ever tried to catch a calf?" Joel asked her.

"No, but that's because men like Reuben Miller and Bishop Joe—experienced wranglers— ride at the back. We girls tend to go in front to show the mothers and calves the way, and the rest of the hands keep the herd from spilling off to the sides and getting lost."

"How many times have you done this?" Lovina estimated the girl to be in her early twenties. "Does everyone start as young as those *Englisch* boys?" She indicated Evan and Jack, who had promised to teach Joel how to rope.

"That's actually why I came over. The boys could use an extra hand to move the cattle into that pen. Think you can do that, Joel?"

Joel looked over at Lovina for permission and his expression—*please, Mamm, please can I?*—made her bite back the words that wanted to fly out of her mouth. *Certainly not—are you batzich?*

"It's up to you, Joel," she forced herself to say, blinking away a sudden terrible vision of him thrown from the saddle and trampled by hundreds of hooves.

He grinned in a way that she hadn't seen since before Mose died. "I can do it, Mamm!"

And almost before he'd finished speaking, his horse responded to the change in his posture and they were off through the sere grass to join the *Englisch* boys. With much pointing and arm waving, the three boys took up positions along an open flank, Joel following their moves and mirroring what they did as intently as he studied arithmetic and geography in the one-room schoolhouse at home.

"He's a good boy," Susan said.

"Most of the time," Lovina agreed.

Silence fell between them, filled with the yips and whistles of the men, the bawling of the calves, the thunder of hooves.

"Do you know the Miller family well?" Susan asked at last.

"I know the relatives in Whinburg Township well," she said. "Our bishop serves their district, too. And Daniel came out our way several years ago to spend the summer. But until this morning I'd never met the rest of the family."

"I thought he might have known you. He seems to have taken quite an interest in Joel. We don't get to see that side of him very often."

There was nothing Lovina could say to this, so she merely smiled.

But Susan seemed to expect a greater response. "He'll make a wonderful father," she said in a confidential tone. "Don't you think? So patient. I heard him telling your boy about the birds and animals he saw."

"I—I suppose so," Lovina managed. Of course he would be a good father. Anyone could see that. What was she getting at? Or was it normal for the women in this district to gossip so freely about their men to near strangers?

"He just needs to see that the right woman is closer than he thinks." Susan glanced sideways at Lovina. "You knew him in the past. What does he like to see in a woman?"

Lovina's mouth fell open. "What do you mean? I haven't seen him in years."

"Just what I say. Does he like a girl who gives her opinions? Or one who's more *demut*, more humble in listening to what he has to say? Every man likes a woman who's a good cook, but what are his favorite things to eat? His favorite color? His favorite song at singing?"

Goodness gracious. She had only met this woman a couple of hours ago and already she was grilling Lovina like a fish. Because of course Lovina knew all those things about Daniel, but she'd rope a calf herself and ride it down the mountain before she'd share a single memory. Not because she was a dog in the manger, but because the past belonged in the past.

"I think any man would be happier with a girl who is just herself, rather than someone who tries to be everything she thinks he wants."

"Is that what you did?"

Lovina stared at her. Who on earth had she been talking to? Daniel would never have confided such a thing.

"When you and your husband were courting," Susan clarified.

Oh. *"Ja,* of course."

"But you do try to please him, don't you? Like any good wife would."

Clearly the gossip had not stretched to the visitors yet, and the details of their lives were still their own. "My husband died last November," Lovina said a little stiffly.

"Oh." Susan's gloved fingers went to her mouth. "I didn't know."

Lovina had to get away. The Miller twins were still on the other side of Joel's cows. There was only one thing to do. "I'm going to see if Malena and Rebecca need a hand."

Rosie was only too happy to obey as Lovina wheeled her around and skirted the perimeter of the huge group of animals. Now she had another reason to dislike Susan Bontrager, she thought grimly as she made her way over to the twins and returned Joel's excited wave.

The girl had forced Lovina to learn to herd cattle.

Chapter 5

THE COWBOYS ATE their packed lunch in two shifts, one group keeping the ever-moving cattle together while the other group bolted down thick roast beef and salad sandwiches and bean pickles and whoopie pies. Joel's new *Englisch* friends spent fifteen minutes teaching him how to rope a standing rock before the first group was whistled up by Evan and Jack's father, the owner of the Star. His young sons, Joshua, and the Troyers led off down the trail. The boys from the Bar Z kept the cattle in order at the sides and rear until the animals realized they were going home and strung themselves out in a trotting walk. Noise and dust boiled into the air in equal measure, but

Lovina had to admit that while it looked chaotic, it was also very well organized.

She was becoming used to the sight of Malena and Rebecca Miller riding and shouting with as much skill as their brothers. Her imagination failed her at what the bishop of their district in Willow Creek would say if he could see Amish girls behaving this way. But really, even she could see that every hand was needed for such an enormous undertaking. An Amish child was taught from birth that everyone, even the smallest animal on the farm, had a job to do. Here, that principle still applied. Today she had learned that there were those who stayed home to cook the massive evening meal for all the people who had come to help, and there were those who did the hard labor of moving cattle during roundup. Both jobs were good, honest work. And truly, if a woman were to become a ranch wife, being able to be a helpmeet in both areas would make her more useful to her husband and the life they were building together for the glory of God.

Not that Lovina could do much to contribute today. But at the moment she was happy to act the part of a fence post with Joel, Susan, and Cousin Joe, creating a physical block as the last two cowboys of the first group vanished down the trail. Their job was to prevent the mothers and calves from rushing the gate and undoing all the work it had taken to separate them.

"Need to give them some space," Cousin Joe said gruffly. "About a mile. Young Joel, close that gate and then I'll show you how to rope something bigger than a rock."

Since his new friends had gone with their father, Joel nodded eagerly and did as he was told. While the horses grazed and drank from the portable stock tank, Lovina walked over to watch. She admired her son's ability to create a loop and even throw it, but on the first throw he learned there was a big difference between a rock and a moving calf, especially one that got spooked at the snaky object flying at it from out of the sky.

"He learns fast," Daniel said from behind her.

Lovina tried not to show that every cell in her body had leaped at the sound of his voice. She turned as naturally as she could. "*Ja*," she agreed. "Faster than either his father or me."

"Want to try it?"

He couldn't be serious, so she treated it as a joke. "*Neh*, I'll leave that to the men," she said lightly. "With my luck, the calf would pull me right out of the saddle and drag me down the mountain."

He chuckled. "Rosie wouldn't let that happen. You'd just lean back, loop the rope around the saddle horn, and she'd do the rest." The brim of his hat shaded his face from the sun, but she could still see the twinkle in his eyes.

Oh my, no. She couldn't allow herself to enjoy his charm. After today, it wasn't likely she'd see him again. That particular gate would be left wide open for Susan.

She turned back to Joel, who made yet another attempt to settle the loop around a calf's neck. It slid off its rump. But instead of giving up, he coiled the stiff rope in the way Cousin Joe instructed, prepared the loop, and tried again on a different animal.

Six tries. Seven. The calves had figured out what he was up to, and were dancing out of range.

"I am amazed," Lovina said. "He is sticking with this. Usually if he can't do something, he gives it up and tries again another day."

"Maybe he knows there won't be another day." Daniel watched for a moment while she absorbed the knowledge that he, too, believed her time on the Circle M would be short. "His arm is good, and so is his eye. He'll get it."

The words were hardly out of his mouth

when the rope slid over the ear of a calf, and it turned just enough for the loop to settle fully over its head. Joel whooped in triumph while Cousin Joe helped him hold the rope.

"What do you do with it once you have it?" Lovina asked, laughing.

"Well, usually you're on horseback and the calf is running away at full speed. Once you have him, you bring him back to the herd so he can find his mother."

"Is that what you're afraid will happen when we go down?"

He shrugged one shoulder. "Happens every season. You get so you can see the signs they're about to run, and try to head them off."

Cousin Joe removed the rope from the bawling calf and while it ran back to its mother, kicking its back hooves in irritation, he waited for Joel to coil the rope properly and showed him how to tie it to his saddle. Then the boy ran over to them. "Did you see, Mamm? I roped him all myself!"

"You did well," Lovina told him. "It looks much harder than roping a rock."

"Evan says they have a bale of hay in the barn with horns tied on it, and they practice all winter."

"We did, too," Daniel told him. "When we were boys, we knew we'd be trailing cattle with Dat, so every chance we got, we practiced. Until Dat fed our bale to the horses. Then we roped each other."

Joel laughed, and Lovina smiled at that enchanting sound twice in one morning. Ah, how it lightened her heart to hear her boy laugh again!

Susan and the twins strolled up, and in the middle of Joel's excited retelling of the story for them, Susan said, "*Ja*, Joel, the first time is always exciting. But now you'd better collect all the trash from our lunches. I see an apple core there where you were eating with the Martin children. Pick it up so it doesn't attract animals."

Joel hesitated, then ran off to do as she asked before Lovina could say a word. "An apple core will do no harm, surely?" she finally managed. "Won't the woodchucks like it?"

"We don't leave litter in the allotments," Susan said firmly. "Isn't that right, Daniel?"

"Not actual litter, no," he said, "but I don't see—"

"Susan's right," Rebecca said. "Joel is doing a good job. He just found a sandwich wrapper that blew into that bush. We care for the land even in the smallest of ways, don't we?"

Daniel could hardly say no, and Susan glowed as though she had received a compliment.

Hmph. The Amish believed that an entire community instructed a child in the way that he should go, so Lovina tried to be gracious about Susan's setting her boy to a task that no one else had been asked to do. Fortunately, nearly all the cowboys were conscientious about packing out what they had packed in, and his task didn't take more than a few minutes.

But Lovina also knew what Daniel's sisters were up to. They wanted a match between him and Susan. Well, she was quite prepared to stand out of the way. If Daniel had managed to stay single all this time only to fall for transparent attempts like this, then he deserved to be roped and tied.

The sun had moved across the meridian into the southwest, and with a squint at how far it had to go, Reuben Miller stuck two fingers in his mouth to give his three sharp whistles. "Moving out!" he shouted as everyone collected their horses and prepared for the last stage of the roundup.

"Lovina, Joel—you're in front with us," Malena called.

Some of the pairs were already on the trail,

which Lovina remembered meant the mothers were experienced and looking forward to the green pastures below. Once she was mounted, she seated her hat firmly and gazed over the collection field for Joel. Where was he? His horse was smaller—surely it wouldn't get lost in this moving sea of cattle. She fell behind, doing her best to shoo the cows into some kind of order as she tried to find her son.

Oh thank goodness, there he was, on the uphill side with Susan.

"Joel, *kumm!*" she called. "In front, with Malena and Rebecca!"

But he couldn't hear her in all the ruckus. Fine, this was as close to the front as she was going to get. She had to keep him within sight, though if anything happened she would have to fight her way across the entire herd to get to him.

And oh goodness, there went two calves away down the slope!

Rosie jerked her head and swerved after them while Lovina hung on for dear life. The horse got in front of the runaways and then cut back and forth to force them to retrace their steps up the slope to join the others.

"*Neh!*" she scolded her horse. "Please don't do that again."

Rosie's ears twitched and Lovina took a better grip on the reins. Naomi had told her the horse would obey, but she had to be firm. Now where was Joel? She had fallen farther behind now. Another cowboy had ridden up to take her place at the shoulder of the herd.

"Joel!" she shouted. Was that an answering shout? "Joel!"

They emerged on to a grassy plateau, with the first of four gates at the far end. One of the twins was already opening it.

"Mamm!"

Oh, thank goodness. In the distance, through a cloud of dust, she could see a small arm waving. He was practically at the rear of the herd, where some of the cattle were still on the trail through the trees, and where the most experienced riders were supposed to be. That Susan had better watch out—she was about to get an earful for not bringing him up front where he belonged.

"Rosie, let's go." She dug her heels in and leaned forward as Malena had taught her, and the horse galloped back, swerving only once to straighten out a couple of calves who might be thinking of making a run for it.

And there was Susan, riding along at the rear of the herd as though there wasn't a thing wrong in all the world. Riding with Cousin Joe and two other cowboys. Lovina's heart plunged. "Susan," she shrieked, "where is Joel?"

"I thought he was with you," the girl called back. "He was circling around to join you a minute ago. What are you doing back here?"

"You've lost my son? Where's Daniel?"

"Chasing calves, where do you think? Lovina—"

"Look out!" Cousin Joe shouted. "That one's going to make a break!"

Rosie juked to the right to stop the calf's flight back up the trail, and Lovina practically came out of the saddle. Two more calves chose that moment to do the same, and fast as greased lightning they were galloping up the trail to the last place they had seen their mothers.

With a yell, Reuben Miller wheeled his horse around and took off after them. Before she was even conscious of doing so, Lovina had bent low over Rosie's back and galloped after him.

Joel was lost. He was not up front, and he was not back here, so that meant that somehow he had been left behind on the trail. She was going to find him, though every steer in Montana stood in her way.

Chapter 6

DANIEL HAD EXPECTED several of the calves to break, but not half a dozen at once, and not when he was distracted by trying to keep Lavina and Joel in sight. But no matter his feelings, he couldn't just leave the animals up here. Without their mothers, they would die from predators, and on top of that, snow was going to fly any day. He could feel it in the air. So he wheeled Marigold around and galloped up the trail after the nearest group.

In the distance, he heard his father whistle, which could only mean that even more calves had followed their bad example. Well, Dat would round them up with Susan's help. Daniel urged Marigold on up the trail, and in less than a

quarter mile, sure enough, there were three rene-
gades circling anxiously behind an outcropping,
clearly lost. He got them moving back down the
trail, though the odds were that the panicked
creatures would turn tail again and he'd meet
them on his way down with the others. With
luck, Dat would be right behind him to collect
them.

Farther up the mountain, he listened for the
telltale crashing in the brush or a desolate
bawling that would tell him where the calf had
gone. Another half mile on, he found one grazing
peacefully among the trees. A single calf was
easily lost, so he roped it and tied it next to the
trail for Dat.

That was four. Two left to go.

The sound of hoofbeats alerted him. This had
to be Dat now. He opened his mouth to hail him,
when Rosie burst around a turn in the trail, going
full tilt up the slope, Lovina low over her back.

He shouted, the calf bolted to the end of its
rope, and at the sight of him and Marigold, Rosie
clattered to a halt.

"Lovina!" He leaped from his horse's back and
grabbed Rosie's throat latch. "Are you all right?
What's going on?"

Her face was dusty, and tears had made tracks

from the corners of her eyes down to her jawline. "Joel," she gasped. "I can't find him."

"He's not with the twins?" He had been riding forward the last Daniel had seen him. What was everyone thinking, to lose track of a small, inexperienced boy?

"He was with Susan. He was trying to come to me, but they lost sight of him. And now he's gone." Her voice wavered and broke. "This was a mistake. We should never have come here." Fresh tears trickled down the tracks the others had made.

"Lovina. Look at me." He released Rosie's harness and put a hand on hers, which had a death grip on the reins.

"We have to find him." Her voice spiralled upward. "Now!"

"And we will. But you have to calm yourself." Rosie was stepping and backing uneasily. "Rosie feels your distress and it's not helping her do her best for you. Breathe."

She took one ragged breath. Then another.

"*Gut,* Lovina. Joel is a smart boy. He's probably gone after a calf. His sense will tell him to come back down to the trail, and that's where we'll meet him. All right?"

"How do you know?" she wailed.

"Because I did the same as a boy. Frightened Mamm half to death, but I was determined to do my part and bring that calf in no matter what. I bet Joel is the same."

"Did you?" Her gray eyes searched his. "Bring it in?"

"Once Dat found me, I did, with his help."

"Oh, he is going to be in so much *Druwwel*." Her voice shook.

"In trouble for frightening you, maybe, but if he brings a calf in, he will have done well, done his part to help. It will be a good and worthy thing."

But her fear would not let her see it that way. "Can we go?"

"*Ja*. But first, we listen."

"For what?"

"For a horse or calf off trail, crashing around in the bush. And for *der himmlischer Vater's* voice, guiding us."

"I've been praying all the way."

"Then He will answer. *Kumm mit*."

He mounted up and she didn't have to encourage Rosie—the horse walked obediently behind Marigold as soon as he urged her into motion. His sharp ears caught the bawl of a calf. "That way."

They were nearly back to the gathering field now, so it would be easy to spot. And a few minutes later there it was, poking its face through the bars of the gate and hollering to be let in, though its mother was miles away.

"Open the gate," he instructed Lovina. "I'll put him in here for now while we have a look for Joel."

"Will he be up this far?" she asked as she rode up and unlatched the gate so that he could drive the calf through.

"If he was after a different calf, chances are good it will have tried to come back here."

"The last place it nursed."

"*Ja*. You're a good student."

"*Neh*, I am terrified that my son is lost on this mountain."

Her voice was rising again, so he brought Marigold close to her horse—close enough that they could clasp hands. Which was not going to happen, he warned himself.

"It may seem like he could be anywhere in the high country, but the fact is, if he rides down, he'll hit a trail somewhere along the way. Or a field, or a gate. All he has to do is follow those to the county road."

"And then what?"

"Well, hopefully he'll remember to ride north, and he'll pass right by the big gate to our lane. It's hard to miss a *Circle M* made out of wrought iron over your head."

She did not smile. "What if he rides south?"

"Then he'll come into Mountain Home, and someone will call Dat to tell us he's there."

Her worried gaze searched his. "You're assuming an awful lot about my boy, Daniel."

"I'm assuming he's smart and resourceful like his *mamm*," he said quietly. "But what I know is that he's curious and observant. He will have noticed these things, even if they weren't familiar. Believe me."

"I'm trying," she said, and her voice broke again.

She was nearly at the end of her tether. He implored God to give them both strength, and for Joel to be guided to them by his Father's loving hand. Then he said, "We'll ride the lower perimeter of the collection field and keep our eyes open for that calf. When we see it, Joel will be right behind it."

But he wasn't. When they did find a second calf, it was drinking from the creek that supplied the stock tank. Lovina called until her voice was hoarse, but they heard nothing but the wind, and saw nothing but clouds covering the lowering sun and two yearling mule deer passing silently through the trees.

The deer were going to their bedding places for the night.

He fought down the cold lump of apprehension forming in his belly. "Lovina, the sun is going down. We can't trail calves in the dark—too dangerous for the horses. We need to get these animals down to the corral, and form a search party."

"You mean leave here? But what if Joel—"

"He's not a calf. If he wasn't chasing this last one, he's probably waiting at one of the gates. We'll check on our way down."

He saw her mouth tighten on the words boiling up out of her. Her hands gripped the reins. She clearly wanted to send Rosie galloping willy-nilly through the woods so she could search for herself.

"Lovina-love." The old nickname came out of nowhere—some door in his heart that he thought was closed forever. "We'll find him. I promise you."

Maybe it was his promise. Maybe it was shock at his slip of the tongue. But she controlled her panic with a visible effort, and turned Rosie so that she could open the gate and let him guide the second calf through it.

He pulled the cell phone out of the inside pocket of his coat, and Dat answered on the first ring.

"Where are you?"

"Gathering field, heading down. We've got two here, one tied on the trail. Is Joel with you?"

His father's silence told Daniel the answer, and the knot in his stomach tightened. "You haven't seen him?" Reuben asked slowly.

"*Neh*. Lovina is with me. Susan?"

"She and one of the Lazy Star boys took eight runaways on to meet up with the others. I'll check all the gates down to the road and meet you at the corral."

His father disconnected. Daniel's eyes met Lovina's and the fear in them sickened him. "Dat's going down to check all the gates. If Joel is waiting, he'll bring him up to meet us at the corral." He phrased it carefully, and her fear receded just a little, to be replaced by hope.

The ride down the trail became a race against the sun, which seemed to fall faster than it ever had. Or maybe it was just that the clouds were moving in more swiftly now, and darkness was gathering fast. They found the third calf still pulling against its rope. Instead of releasing it, Daniel used the rope like a lead line, and the others went along with it as Lovina brought up the rear. Three miles of trail seemed like a nightmare that would never end, especially as the temperature dropped. They reached the last field in twilight, barely able to see the bars of the portable corral. By the time the runaway calves were in it, darkness had gathered under the pines and there was barely enough light in the meadow to see.

The gate at the entrance to the meadow clanged shut.

"Mamm!" a piping voice called. "Mamm!"

A sound came from Lovina's throat that Daniel hoped never to hear again in his life.

Two riders came toward them, the smaller one with a fourth calf on the lead line tied to his saddle.

"I got him, Mamm! All myself. It took me hours and hours, but I roped him!"

As she pulled her son from the saddle and into her arms, Lovina burst into wrenching sobs—the kind that came in the morning after enduring the dark watches of the night.

Chapter 7

LOVINA COULD NOT STOP SHAKING. She would have held Joel in her arms for the rest of eternity if he had not wriggled out of them to obey Reuben Miller.

"We must unsaddle the horses," the older man told him as he loosened his gelding's cinch. "If we are going to stay here for the night, we want Del and the others to be comfortable."

"Del is a funny name for a horse," Joel said.

"He doesn't care for Delphinium." Reuben took in Lovina and Daniel with a glance. "I've already called to tell Naomi. They will be having a good dinner without us. But we will have ours tomorrow, when we get home."

"And tonight?" Lovina asked. She had spent

the last couple of hours in such terrible fear that the thought of eating made her ill. But Joel must have something.

"I don't need to eat," Daniel said, busy on the other side of his horse. "But I have half a sandwich in my pack that you and Joel are welcome to."

"No need," Reuben said. "When has your mother ever let us go on roundup without a backup plan? We have trail packs with tents and sleeping mats. And she has put enough food in my backpack for a *gut* supper. Joel, I will take care of your Bachelor Button if you will collect firewood and kindling. The fire ring and camping place are over there, in that level spot."

In the last of the light, they set up camp, putting the tack inside the tents in case the weather kept its promise, and the horses in the corral. And while the chicken salad sandwiches were squashed and a little watery because of the pickles, they and the slightly flattened apple cake had never tasted so good to Lovina. Or perhaps it was that Joel was leaning against her, safe and warm, the firelight flickering over his dear features. It wasn't long after he'd finished his last bite that his weight grew heavy and it was time to carry him the few feet to the tent and put him to bed.

Daniel had zipped two down sleeping bags together for them. "It's going to be cold," he'd said simply, but she wondered if somehow he had known that she would need to hold her boy through the night, reassuring herself every time she woke that he was safe against her chest.

Reuben followed suit soon after, in the tent he would share with his own son, leaving Daniel and Lovina with cold backs and warm fronts as they huddled on stumps, so close to the flames that the toes of their boots nearly rested in the ashes. She should go in the tent, too. But she had something that must be said before she lost her nerve.

"Reuben," she said in the direction of his tent, "*denkes* for bringing my son back to me."

"No thanks needed," came the gruff voice from inside. "The boy did well, waiting at the gate with the calf where it had been grazing, instead of dragging it up the trail to try to find us."

"Just as Daniel thought he might." Lovina glanced to the side, where Daniel was gazing into the fire.

"*Guder nacht,*" Reuben said pointedly, and they heard the *scritch* of the nylon bag as he burrowed, fully clothed, into it.

"Will you laugh at me if I wear my down coat when I sleep?" she said in a low tone to Daniel. "I want Joel wrapped inside it, like a baby kangaroo in its mother's pocket."

"I was going to suggest that you do," he said. "Dat probably has his on, too. I'll put mine over me like a quilt. I'm a pretty warm sleeper."

She had no business thinking about that at all. She turned the subject instead. "Even when it's nearly freezing?"

"The bags are warm. No one is going to freeze tonight. Just keep your head covered."

"I'm beginning to believe that when you say something, it's usually right."

He chuckled. "Not always."

I thought you loved me.

Like an echo, the words he'd said the night he proposed came back to her. Even all these years later, she felt herself blush. He had been right, then. She had loved him. But there were things that overrode love, that made the sacrifice of it necessary, though nothing had ever hurt so much.

Suddenly it seemed important that he know about those things. Especially since the sound of his father's breathing told her he had fallen asleep almost at once.

"Daniel, that night on the bridge—"

"This is no time to talk about it." He got up and turned his back to the fire.

She rose and did the same. Maybe this was better. Her low voice would go out into the dark, not toward the two tents.

"There were things—reasons—for my saying what I did that I never had the chance to explain."

"I don't think those things matter now, Lovina."

"But I think they do," she said urgently. "I've let you believe whatever you believe for all this time. I want to make it right. So that at least you believe the truth."

"You didn't tell me the truth that night?"

She hesitated. "Not all of it."

His shoulders heaved in a deep sigh. "Whatever either of us believes doesn't change anything. You made the choice you thought was right, and I accepted it. End of story."

"But it isn't the full story. Please, Daniel."

He turned back to the fire, which had burned so low all he had to do was kick it down and it would go out with no danger of spreading out of its shallow pit to the grass.

"You'll be going back to the Wengerd place tomorrow, and catching a train after that, if it doesn't snow. It's not likely we'll see each other again. Let's just leave the past in the past, where it belongs."

She wanted to protest, to grab his sleeve and shake it until he listened, but that would wake Reuben. So instead, she wished him good night, ducked into her tent, zipped it up behind her, and slipped into the sleeping bag next to Joel. He murmured and snuggled against her in his sleep.

No matter how much she wanted to speak, to make Daniel believe her reasons had been just, she would just have to accept that he didn't want to hear them. And really, what would have happened if she had said yes that night instead of no? The *gut Gott* would not have given her Joel, and what would her life be without him?

He was her comfort and her joy.

But even with that knowledge, it was a long time before Lovina could get comfortable enough to fall asleep. And if the soft sounds of a man turning over again and again next door were any indication, she wasn't the only one.

———

JOSHUA COULD HAVE TAKEN off and hightailed it away from the ranch the moment the mother-and-calf pairs were safely in the home field and the gate closed behind them. With the clouds of dust, the bawling cattle and the crowd of shouting, whooping neighbors, it would have been easy to put his heels to his horse and head out through the woods to get the night started.

Dat was up on the mountain. He'd never know. But Josh did owe his horse better than that.

He finished his work, helping the other cowboys funnel the rest of the animals into the big field. Then he took the time to untack Sandy (he was *not* going to call him Chrysanthemum in front of the other guys) and give him a rubdown and a bucket of oats before he turned him out in the horse pasture to enjoy a good graze after all his labors.

Josh was done with labor and ready for a good graze himself, and it wouldn't be at the house with the half Amish, half *Englisch* crowd, either. On the good side, the chaos at the Circle M concealed his escape. On the bad side, he couldn't go into the house to take a shower and clean up. One of his sisters or Mamm would catch him for sure, and he'd be stuck with yet more chores. Luckily his friends helped each other out in that department.

As the guys from the Rocking Diamond dude

ranch rode into the yard, as dusty and covered in manure and mud as he was, he caught Chance Madison's eye. Chance gave a subtle nod and a grin as he and his dad's hands rode down the lane. Most of them would be back in an hour, showered and spit shined, for dinner. Mamm's cooking was legendary, and none of the cowboys missed the big roundup dinner on the Circle M if they could help it. Not even the fancy chef at the Rocking Diamond could hold a candle to her, though they paid him a fortune and the folks from New York and Los Angeles raved.

But there was more to life than cooking.

On foot, he shouldered his little backpack with his *Englisch* clothes in it and cut through the woods to the county highway. In just a few minutes, he heard the Rocking Diamond horses, ambling along and probably ready for their own barns. Chance came up behind him, offered him a hand, and he swung up to ride postillion for the mile or so they had to go.

The dude ranch was massive, bigger even than the Circle M. Josh supposed that in order to pay the equally massive mortgage, the Madisons had to diversify. The place was a working ranch, a retreat center, a dude ranch, and if none of those suited, you could rent yourself a cabin just to sit out on your little porch and enjoy the view and the chef's two-course breakfast, delivered to your door. But at ten thousand dollars a week per couple, the ranch made most of its money on folks who wanted to learn ranch work. Some were serious about it. Some just wanted something different to put on their Instagram feeds. And Chance had even mentioned the other day that a movie company had called wanting to know when the tourists tended to clear out. Some actor wanted privacy to learn how to rope and ride so he could do his own stunts for a movie.

"My sister says the folks in Morgan checked out and Housekeeping hasn't been in yet," Chance reported after they dismounted, his phone in his hand. "You go clean up, while I put this good boy away." He patted his horse's neck.

All the cabins were named after breeds of horses, though Josh doubted there was a Morgan horse in all of Lincoln County. But he wasn't fussy—the water was hot and there was lots of it. Even a clean white bath towel that hadn't been used. Chance, of course, showered in his own room at the big house. But the fewer people who saw Josh here, the better. Fifteen minutes later, he had hiked over the shoulder of the hill and was back on the highway, where the rumble of Chance's big Ford F450 caught up to him.

He vaulted inside and they were off.

"Where to?" Chance straight-armed the wheel and asked the question like there was any other answer.

"Whitefish," Josh joked.

"You wish. Talley's it is."

Talley's was the bar in Mountain Home where a lot of the guys from the ranches hung out after their work was done. It was dim and loud and the beer was crafted right there. It was the best-kept secret in the county, and the cowboys aimed to keep it that way. The girls came over from Libby and some of the other towns and between shooting the breeze and dancing and playing the dozen different kinds of video games they had ranged along the walls, you could spend half the night there without even trying.

Josh rarely tried. It just happened.

Tyler Carson already had a table saved, big enough for them and a trio of girls who had become regulars since the youngest one had turned twenty-one. Chance was twenty-two, and Ty had had his twenty-first birthday in the summer, so he was still in the honeymoon phase where he got blasted by nine o'clock. No self-control, that was

Ty's problem. Which was usually when Josh pried the keys to their car out of his hand and became the designated driver for whoever could cram into the car and go back to Ty's to party. His parents never cared who came over, and as long as you could still walk a straight line when you got in your car, they didn't care how much of their stock you drank, either.

Josh had scrimped and saved for three years to buy this car. He rubbed the steering wheel affectionately as they drove back to the Carson house. It was a beauty—a 1969 Dodge Dart, the one they called the Swinger. Okay, it was more Bondo than metal, but the motor ran like a champ and it could blister a trail of rubber down the highway better than Chance's truck, even. Josh had studied for the Montana driver's test, hiding the booklet out in the tack room with the rest of his stuff, and passed it the first time. Their agreement was that he'd buy the car, and Ty would pay for the insurance, store it, and keep it maintained. He worked at the auto parts store in Libby, so he got a good discount on parts.

Chance and the other guys from the ranch had gone on to Libby, being as it was Saturday night. Now, Ty was trying to sing "Red Solo Cup" in the backseat, his arms around a girl on either side and some kid one of them knew crammed up against the window. Josh drove as carefully as his buzz would let him while he tucked the youngest girl against his ribs. She smelled good. Not as nice as Carey, who smelled like wildflowers. He hadn't seen her in a while. Since summer? He tried to think, and couldn't remember.

He remembered her scent, though. And how soft her skin was. How loud her laugh and how she called him Joshie.

"Where's Carey these days?" came out of his mouth in the middle of the girls' conversation about some science fiction series that was streaming, to which he couldn't contribute much. They all agreed that they were crazy about the lead actor, whose name meant nothing to him.

"Carey Lindholm?" The girl beside him yawned. "I heard she got accepted to U of M in Missoula. Starts in January."

"Overachievers Anonymous," one of the girls in the back said. "I hate her."

"Yup, she's too good for us now," the third one said. "Haven't seen her for months. Shut up, Ty. You sound like a sick cow."

"Hey," he said, hurt. "My grandma says I'm a great singer."

"Your grandma isn't here," she said, crushing him into silence.

His parents weren't there, either, Joshua saw as he pulled into the yard. "Where's your folks, Ty?"

"'S a long weekend, Amish boy," Ty slurred. "They went to the cabin."

"Lucky them. I'd love a cabin on Flathead Lake." The girl beside him slid out as he put the Dart in park. "C'mon, let's see what's in the liquor cabinet so Joshie can have a good time, too."

"Don't call me that," he said, frowning.

"Joshie—Joshie—Joshie needs a washie," she sang, and fell up the porch steps.

He rolled his eyes and hauled her to her feet. He remembered now why he'd preferred Carey to her friends. But once he'd lowered the level of the bottle of Canadian Club a little, he didn't care anymore, and soon he and she were tangled up on Ty's sofa downstairs and nothing mattered at all.

———

IN THE MORNING, the sun had barely lit the rocky peaks of the mountain behind them when Daniel had Del and Marigold saddled and Dat had taken down their tent and stowed everything in the trail bags. The clouds had kept their promise and the snow had started sometime in the night. Already there was an inch in the meadow, crisscrossed with bird and animal tracks, and trampled to mud in the corral where the calves crowded the gate at the sight of them.

Joel popped out of the tent, looking rumpled and alert, jamming his hat down over hair that stood on end. Lovina climbed out behind him, her hair hastily wound up under the *Duchly* and her skirt wrinkled. He had never seen her first thing in the morning, and it took him a moment to recover from eyes that looked larger because of her pale cheeks. She hadn't slept much, either. His fault, probably, since he'd been so ungracious last night, cutting her off and walking away. But hearing her talk about the night on the bridge over Willow Creek, when the fireflies had made constellations of beauty in the fields on either side and the sound of the water rushing below had whispered, *Ask her—ask her ... ach,* it had been too much for him to take.

"We need to get these calves back home to their mothers," Dat said. "While it is the Lord's Day, I don't think He will fault us for finishing our task. However, we will take a few minutes to give thanks to *der himmlischer Vater* for keeping us through the night."

Daniel schooled his jumbled thoughts to stillness, focusing on his breath condensing on the chilly air and how thankful he was that God had preserved them, their horses, and these last calves from the dangers of the night. Reuben offered up his prayer as solemnly as he might have in church, where he was deacon, and not standing in a partially frozen field with curious horses looking on and hungry calves bawling in the background.

When Reuben had concluded, he lifted his head and said to Lovina, "Daniel and I will help you tear down and saddle up, and then we'll let the animals out. You and Joel will lead, and we'll close the gate and come behind."

The trail under the belt of pines downslope had no snow yet, but by the time they'd ridden the last mile and emerged through the final gate on to the county road, another inch had accumulated in the open spaces. The road itself was still clear, but it wouldn't be long. Rosie and Button set a good pace, no doubt anxious to get back to their warm barn and a good meal. Daniel watched Lovina's straight back and marveled that a woman who had never ridden a saddle horse could now look almost comfortable. Then again, her whole being seemed at ease now that Joel was riding beside her.

Could he have given her even more peace by taking the time to listen to what she had to say last night?

Never mind. What was done was done. And if he had regretted it between brief snatches of sleep, well, he would keep that to himself.

Joel whooped as they drove the calves in through the gates of the Circle M, and while Reuben and Daniel moved them into the field where the other pairs grazed and helped them mother up, Lovina and Joel rode to the barn. By the time Daniel and his father had put their own horses away and double-checked that all was well with Rosie and Button, Lovina and Joel had bathed and changed and Joel was regaling the rest of the family with the story of their night in the wilderness.

Though they would have eaten breakfast hours ago, Naomi and the twins had wasted no time in getting another on the table for them. Daniel wolfed down waffles covered in syrup, sausages, eggs, and good, old-fashioned scrapple. And all the while, he watched the color return to Lovina's face and the sparkle to her eyes as she laughed. Adam was in the middle of telling Joel the story of the blizzard four years ago, which had snowed them in for several days before the county could clear the roads out this far, when the kitchen door opened and Joshua came in looking as though he had spent the night on the mountain, too.

"Is that breakfast?" he said as though he couldn't believe his luck.

A faint whiff of something that could have been either bad breath or a mix of cigarettes and alcohol—or all three—wafted past Daniel. Their mother's face scrunched up in distaste, and Reuben's enjoyment of his meal appeared to sizzle away.

Josh took his place and began loading his plate, shoveling in the food as though he hadn't eaten since breakfast yesterday.

"Are you just getting home?" Daniel asked in disbelief.

Joshua looked up from his waffles. "Aren't you?"

"We spent the night at the corral. Were you chasing runaways?"

Joshua shook his head, keeping his mouth too full to talk.

Malena rolled her eyes. "He's been in town."

When her youngest brother glared at her, she said, "Don't give me that face. I saw that red truck from the dude ranch go by with you in it after we rode in yesterday."

Mamm got up to get the coffee pot, and filled their cups. "Joshua, you know how much it grieves me when you go out with those worldly boys." She put up her free hand when he opened his mouth to protest. "I know. *Rumspringe*. But that doesn't hide a multitude of sins. Or the smell of smoke and alcohol. You should be ashamed, coming home in this shape on the Lord's Day, especially when we have company."

"I didn't know they were still here," he mumbled into his coffee cup.

Dat laid down his fork, the ting of metal on the china plate loud in the silence. "It's *gut* to know that you have time on your hands, son. That means you'll be able to clean all the tack tomorrow."

"All—"

"The saddles and bridles of the cutting horses," their father said calmly. "Adam and Zach will be checking the pairs today, making sure no one has any injuries from the trail. On Tuesday you can add theirs to your list."

"But Dat, I was going to—"

"You're not going off the ranch. None of us are. Unless I miss my guess, there'll be a foot of snow on the ground by midafternoon."

"Lucky thing the pantry's full," Rebecca said.

"Could I borrow a phone?" Lovina said. "I wonder if Cousin Joe could come get us before it gets too deep?"

But Cousin Joe couldn't. One of his cows had developed an infection from a cut when she'd rubbed up against a fence nail, and he had to wait for the vet, who didn't appreciate being called out on a Sunday. His boys had their hands full with the herd, doing the same job as Daniel's brothers.

By midafternoon, Naomi looked at the snow whirling past the windows and took charge. "You'll just have to stay with us until this blizzard passes and it's safe for a buggy to go out again, Lovina."

"But how long will that be?" Lovina asked. Daniel was in the mud room putting on his boots, and could hear her clearly. "Can the train leave from Libby? Or the bus?"

"Hard to say," Naomi replied. "I don't know about the train, but the county is pretty good about the roads. But if it gets worse than Reuben predicts, it could be a few days before anyone can get you over to the bishop's, never mind into town."

"But our clothes—our things. I can't borrow from you folks forever."

"Daniel will ride out and get them."

Daniel had already come to the same decision, but ... what was his mother up to?

"Oh, I couldn't let him do that. Poor Marigold has had a hard enough couple of days."

"We have other horses. Daniel?" Naomi called.

"Already on my way, Mamm," he said, pulling his coat off the rack and settling his hat on his head. "I was going to check for leaks in my house, but I can do that when I get back."

"*Neh*, I can't possibly let you," Lovina protested. "You go check your house. Joel and I can walk. It can't be two miles."

"You just sit down and let us look after you," Naomi said firmly. "It's one thing to send Daniel out—he knows his way. But I'm not sending a woman and a child out into this weather, and strangers to Montana to boot. No, you just make yourself comfortable. We're happy to have you. And goodness knows we need to show better hospitality than a cold night out on the open range."

As Daniel went out the back door and headed

toward the barn, he heard Lovina make a forlorn sound of frustration.

He couldn't blame her. He felt the same way. The last thing in the world he wanted was to be snowbound with his entire family ... and the woman who had refused to become a part of it.

Chapter 8

"LUCKY FOR YOU LOVINA TRAVELS LIGHT," Little Joe said. He patted Columbine's rump, where he and Daniel had rigged a yoke of sorts across the back of her saddle and hung the two small rolling suitcases from it like saddle bags. "I've seen tourists come to the dude ranch down the road with half their houses in suitcases and boxes, like they think they'll never see civilization again."

"She and Joel and the Troyers were in a seven-seater van," Daniel pointed out. "I can't imagine there was a lot of room for luggage. What's happened to the Troyers, anyway? I didn't see them when I rode past the house. Surely they didn't go to town in this weather."

"Not in a buggy, they didn't. I suppose you didn't hear."

"Hear what? Did something happen?"

"They skedaddled yesterday as soon as we got home. Their driver was waiting here with his van all fixed and they loaded up and took off."

"You're joking," Daniel said, his mouth agape as he stared at the bishop over Columbine's back. "You mean they've left Lovina and Joel behind and gone home? Why didn't they tell her?"

"You all were up the mountain," Joe said simply. "Turns out Barb Troyer's mother had a heart attack day before yesterday. We found out as soon as we got down the trail. It was just lucky that van got fixed so fast. They'll be in Wyoming by now."

"Huh." Daniel's mind was working through his astonishment. "So now you'll have room for the Lapps until the blizzard goes through and the roads are cleared."

"We might have room, but not much else. We'll leave things as they are, if Naomi wishes it. You have younger folk up there to keep Joel busy, and more women for company for Lovina."

Was the entire district in cahoots to keep Lovina and Joel on the Circle M? "But—"

"We'll look for you all in church next week at

Bontragers' place," Joe said. "With Council Meeting the Sunday after that, we'll all have the opportunity to get our hearts right with God and our brothers and sisters, eh?"

"*Ja,* we will," Daniel agreed, because there was nothing else he could say, and mounted up. "Stay warm."

The bishop laughed at the Rocky Mounain farewell and slapped the horse's rump so that she set off briskly out the barn doors and down the Wengerd lane. The makeshift panniers seemed to be stable, so Daniel let her set the pace while the snow whirled down around them. Little Joe Wengerd might have the arms of a blacksmith, a voice like an avalanche, and no tact at all, but God had chosen him to find the long piece of paper in his hymnbook ten years ago, after old Bishop Bontrager, Susan's *Daadi*, had passed away. The Lord knew that despite appearances, Joe had the heart of a shepherd, even though the task God had set him sometimes made him weep. Oh yes, he had confessed it freely in church, which only went to show how humble his heart truly was.

They came out on the county road and despite the fact that the snow had covered the blacktop six inches deep, Columbine picked up her pace.

With examples like his father and his bishop, a

man could count himself blessed. If only Joshua could see it. Daniel sighed. What was it going to take for his youngest brother to realize that jumping the fence wouldn't put him on the road to happiness? At least he was safe at home for now, and not stranded in town with who knew what so-called friends. The first blizzard of the season would make sure everyone stayed put.

Including their unexpected company.

When he'd put Columbine away and brought in the small suitcases, he couldn't tell which emotion was uppermost in Lovina's face—gratitude or embarrassment.

"Thank you so much, Daniel, for going to all this trouble," she said, her eyes cast down and her cheeks flaming. "I'll be out of your way just as soon as I'm able."

"About that," he said, and told her, Naomi, and the twins about the Troyers and the heart attack.

All the hot color faded from Lovina's face. "They've gone?" she said blankly. "They've left Joel and me here by ourselves?"

"Not exactly by yourselves," Rebecca said cheerfully. "You've got all of us."

Now she blushed again. "I know, and I'm so grateful. I only meant—"

"We know what you meant," Naomi told her reassuringly. "But it is a wonder that they didn't at least call someone here to let you know. I suppose they were so upset by the news that they didn't think."

"What's done is done," Daniel said.

"If they hadn't gone when they did, they wouldn't have been able to go at all," Rebecca pointed out, waving a hand toward the window. "Not in this weather. So maybe for the family's sake it was for the best."

"Mamm, where have you put Lovina?" Daniel hefted the suitcases. "I'll take the bags upstairs."

"I wish your house was done, so that all you boys could bunk there together. For now, Adam is in with Joshua, and Zach will share with you. Lovina and Joel will have the twin beds in their room."

Daniel nodded and took the bags to the end room. It had a nice view out over the trees to the pond—or it would when the snow stopped. At the moment the window showed only a whirling rectangle of white.

"Denki, Daniel," came a quiet voice from behind him. "For bringing our things."

She stood in the doorway, her hands clasped

in front of her. She wore her heart-shaped Lancaster County *Kapp,* a stark contrast with the black of her widow's dress, cape, and apron.

"It was no trouble. I took Columbine—she's sure-footed and I wasn't certain how much ice I'd find. Little Joe and I rigged a yoke to carry the bags."

"That was smart. I was wondering how you would do it. They weren't the kind with a strap that you could just sling over your shoulder."

"I hope you won't take offense about the Troyers," he said awkwardly. "It sounds like the situation was urgent, and the van driver was waiting in the yard as though God had brought him there in the nick of time."

"I have no reason to be offended," she said. Very properly, she didn't enter the bedroom with him in it, standing there by the window at the foot of the twin beds. "Joel and I are well looked after, and I hope I can lend a hand wherever I'm needed."

"There won't be much to do once my brothers and Dat are finished checking the cattle. Unless your name is Joshua." He grinned. "His work is cut out for him tomorrow."

"Maybe Joel could help him. It would be good for him to learn something new each day."

What good would knowing how to clean riding tack be once the boy went back to Whinburg Township? But he didn't say that out loud. "It would be good for Joshua to teach him. Keep him from sulking out there in the barn."

"It worries your parents, his *Rumspringe*?"

"*Ja*. He's in with a rowdy crowd, and there doesn't seem to be any end in sight." Daniel toyed with the single blue curtain, which was backed with insulation like all the drapes in the house, to add to the effectiveness of the double-paned windows. "Sometimes they go down to Kalispell and we don't see him for a couple of days."

She huffed out a breath. "Mine seems so tame in comparison. Buying a worldly bathing suit to go swimming. Riding a bicycle instead of a scooter. Shocking."

He must not think of her swimming in Willow Creek, lithe as a fish.

"I pretty much forgot mine," he confessed. "Too much work. I joined church after I got back from—" He stopped. Were all of their conversations going to return to that summer, like horses to their barn? What was the point?

"Yes, I did, too. And married." She raised her head. "Daniel—"

"I'd better see how the boys are doing with

our calves." She backed into the hall as he passed her, and he caught the scent of floral shampoo and sun-dried cotton.

The same scent that he was quite certain he'd smelled in his dreams for months after he'd come home from Pennsylvania.

———

LOVINA OPENED Joel's suitcase and hung up his little shirts in the space in the closet that had been made for them. It was abundantly clear that Daniel did not want to hear a word from her about the past. The door had closed, and she must accept that he was not interested in her reasons for turning down his proposal, as much as she wanted him to understand.

She hung up her three dresses slowly. She hoped he and his siblings appreciated how much God had given them in their parents and their home. Imagine how different life would have been if, as a child, she had had both! If Mamm and Dat had not died that winter, leaving her to be passed among the family to keep her out of the hands of Child Protective Services. If she had not been taken in for good by Onkel Elmer and Aendi Grace, who had six children already and could barely scratch a living from the soil. She, small and fearful, had disappeared in the crowd, her only consolation the barn cats and the skinny chickens.

Unpacking was completed in less than five minutes, and when she returned to the kitchen, now fragrant with the scent of dinner cooking, Daniel was gone.

"The boys should be back soon," Naomi said. "It will be dark by five. Do you like chicken and dumplings?"

Lovina smiled. "I sure do. It was my husband's favorite. He used to say eating my dumplings was like eating clouds. I would tell him thunder clouds couldn't be that good for his stomach, and he would laugh."

"Maybe you'd make them for us?" Naomi suggested, and together they got to work.

Malena went down to the basement pantry for beet pickles, and Rebecca sliced carrots and made a corn salad.

It was difficult to believe these girls were twins—one freckled and with curly brown hair, the other slight with straight hair twisted prettily on either side of her face and tucked up into her *Kapp*.

"What did your husband do for a living?" Rebecca asked a little shyly, as though she feared Lovina might not like talking about him.

But the time for tears was over. "Mose kept a shop in Whinburg, selling antiques and old farm equipment to the tourists."

"He didn't farm?" Naomi asked in surprise.

"*Neh*, his three brothers had the family farm, but he had no desire to buy in with them. He liked talking to people, driving the spring wagon around the county to yard sales and estate sales."

"And he could make a living doing that?" Rebecca sounded amazed. "The *Englisch* sure like other people's old things, don't they?"

"Some of it turned out to be quite valuable, like the quilt one of our elderly sisters had in her attic," Lovina told her. "Turns out it was made in the seventeen hundreds, and a collector bought it for twenty thousand dollars."

Rebecca dropped her knife with a clatter. "Sorry," she said, picking it up. "How did your husband know it was that old?"

"He didn't. There was a book in the library and he looked it up. Apparently you can date fabrics by their patterns and dyes. This collector came all the way from Pittsburgh and made Mose an offer on sight."

"Wow," Rebecca said, her eyebrows practically up to her hairline.

"It was a windfall, all right," Lovina said, dropping her dumplings by fat tablespoons into the bubbling pot. "Kept us for a year. But that was the largest sale he ever made. Mostly it's just everyday things, like wooden bedsteads and lanterns and such."

"Lanterns?" Malena came up the stairs in time to hear. "Like these I just filled?"

Three lanterns stood waiting on a side table for when supper was over, but at the moment the hissing Coleman lamp hanging from the ceiling gave all the light they needed and more.

"Yes. The *Englisch* think they're quaint, especially the old ones with the etched glass, like that." She nodded toward the one on the windowsill, next to someone's songbook. "Anyway, after he died I took over the shop. I don't have his eye for antiques, but I'm learning."

"Who is looking after things while you're away?"

"His sisters," Lovina replied. "Ruth and Alma take turns and bring the younger children in while the older are in school. Goodness knows there are plenty of toys to play with, and wooden blocks and dolls. My sisters-in-law keep an eye on the papers and the Internet at the library as well, watching for these yard sales, so I don't have to."

"They use the Internet?" Malena said, exchanging a glance with Rebecca. "Your cousin the bishop would never allow that, even though the nearest branch of the library is just over in Libby."

"Our bishop allows us to use it if it's business related," Lovina said. "Something happened a few years ago in Willow Creek where the *Dokterfraa* used the Internet to reunite a family. After that, the church elders decided that the Internet was similar enough to the newspapers that it could be used in a limited way, as long as it didn't come into the home, of course."

"Of course." Naomi nodded. "Our elders here have a similar rule about cell phones. Communication for safety, and for business. None of this swimming nonsense."

"Surfing, Mamm," Malena corrected her with a giggle. "Web *surfing*."

"Surfing, swimming, whatever it's called, it's not allowed," their mother said firmly, while the girls broke out in laughter.

Lovina couldn't help a smile as she stirred the

chicken and dumplings. She tried to imagine her teenaged self talking to Aendi Grace like this. And failed.

These innocent girls, she thought. They have no idea how blessed they are.

Chapter 9

AFTER SUNDAY DINNER AND DISHES, the family went into the big living room. Every Amish family provided a place for worship large enough to accommodate the whole *Gmee*, whether that was a living room, an equipment shed, or a barn loft. Even in building a home, *Gott* came first, then the family's needs second.

From the front windows of the Miller home, on a clear day Daniel could see all the way down the valley to the west pasture. Once he moved into his own home, he would be able to see the lights of his parents' house and they would be able to see his, shining out in companionship with one another. If it were left up to Dat, each of his children would build somewhere on the ranch and they would never be separated. However, Dat also knew that wasn't very practical. Any one of his brothers might decide to go to Kentucky or Ohio or Indiana to look for a bride, and a young man who came out to work as a ranch hand might steal one of his sisters away. His sisters had done a little courting, but the local boys didn't seem to suit either of them.

It was only a matter of time, though, he was sure. Look at Mamm and Dat. They had been neighbors all their lives until one day, the sun came up differently. Or the wind blew in a different direction. Something had happened, Mamm had once said with a faraway smile, that made her see Reuben Miller in a different light. And here they were.

"Lovina," Mamm said as she made herself comfortable in her usual armchair, "on off Sundays we usually take turns reading from the Bible. Do you or Joel have a favorite passage we might read?"

Dat took down the thick *hoch Deutsch* Bible and sat in his chair with the massive book in his lap. The Amish tended to read and correspond in English, and speak *Deitsch* at home and among themselves, of course, but high German was reserved for worship and for Sunday night reading.

"I think Psalm 139 is appropriate for us tonight." Lovina looked down at Joel. "You'll help me, *ja?*"

He nodded, and Dat began to read. After two verses, he passed it to Mamm, who did the same, and then Daniel. Joel was sitting next to him. He handed over the holy book so that he, too, might read some of the most beautiful words in any language, and pointed to the place where he should start. Solemnly, the little boy read:

> *"Wo soll ich hin gehen vor*
> *deinem Geist,*
> *und wo soll ich hin fliehen vor*
> *deinem Angesicht?*
> *Führe ich gen Himmel, so bist*
> *du da.*
> *Bettete ich mir in die Hölle,*
> *siehe, so bist du auch da."*

> *Whither shall I go from thy*
> *spirit?*
> *or whither shall I flee from thy*
> *presence?*
> *If I ascend up into heaven,*
> *thou art there:*

if I make my bed in hell, behold,
thou art there.

When he stopped and looked up at his mother, Lovina smiled with approval and encouragement as she took the book into her lap. Daniel had barely recovered from that smile—which wasn't even directed at him—when she began to read his favorite part in a low voice. To his ears, it sounded like music.

> *"Nähme ich Flügel der Morgen-*
> *röte und bliebe am äußersten*
> *Meer,*
> *so würde mich doch deine Hand*
> *daselbst führen und deine*
> *Rechte mich halten."*

> *If I take the wings of the morn-*
> *ing, and dwell in the utter-*
> *most parts of the sea;*
> *Even there shall thy hand lead*
> *me, and thy right hand shall*
> *hold me.*

Daniel couldn't think of a more appropriate choice of a psalm to give both comfort and hope.

For Lovina, he was pretty certain, Montana was the nearest thing to the uttermost parts of the sea she ever planned to visit in her life. It was *gut* that she was here with his family. Maybe it would help her to feel safe, to see that even in a blizzard, it wasn't so frightening out here. And then when she finally boarded that train to leave, she would feel as though she'd had an adventure, not lived through a disaster.

The thought of her and Joel on that train platform hollowed out his stomach.

Because he was a fool.

He did his best to focus on the voices of his brothers and sisters, and Dat's reading of one of the stories from the *Martyr's Mirror*, but it wasn't easy. And when, exhausted, he banked the wood stove in the basement and climbed the stairs to bed, her soft voice echoed in his memory.

Thy right hand shall hold me.

———

IN THE MORNING, the first thing he and Zach did was go to the window to see if the snow had stopped. Of course it hadn't. The snowflakes whirled down out of the darkness into the golden square of lamplight from the kitchen downstairs.

He couldn't see how much had accumulated, but he'd bet Dat was right about twelve inches at least.

"It would be too much to hope that it would have stopped," Zach said, turning away to put his clothes on.

"Got plans?"

"Checking calves is easier when you can see them."

True enough. "At least Josh will have nothing to complain about. He gets to spend the day in a warm barn."

Zach chuckled as he did up the snaps on his gray shirt and shrugged his suspenders over his shoulders. "He'll learn someday that everything you do has consequences. Especially when Dat is involved."

"He is pretty hard on him," Daniel admitted, pulling on a fresh pair of hand-knitted socks.

"He was hard on all of us—but I can see now that he was fair. And honestly, I wouldn't have it any other way. I feel sorry for young Joel, losing his father. I hope he has someone like Dat in his life."

Daniel couldn't help wondering that himself. "Ask Lovina."

"Doesn't matter," Zach said, going to the door.

"None of our business. All we can do is our best for *der Kind* while he's here, *ja?*"

Zach swung out the door before Daniel could answer.

After a silent grace at the table, and during the clatter and chatter of breakfast, he sneaked a glance or two at Lovina. She'd wakened rough yesterday, but this morning she looked rested, and her color was good. Joel was a bundle of energy, and when he found out he was going to learn how to clean riding tack, he could hardly wait to get started.

"I'd never been in a saddle before Saturday," he said eagerly to Joshua as they put on their boots. "Are they hard to clean?"

"Nope, just time consuming," Josh said, refusing to look at his father. "But I guess until this snow lets up, we have nothing but time, *nix?*"

"Can I come, too, to see the barn?" Lovina asked. She looked over her shoulder at Naomi. "I'll be back soon to help with the dishes."

But Naomi waved her away. "There will always be more dishes. You go, and don't get lost in this blizzard."

Daniel would go along, too, to get the snow shovel. It was time to start clearing decks and walks.

"She didn't mean that, did she?" Joel, muffled up to the eyes in a scarf under his flat-brimmed black felt hat, bounced along beside him as they made their way outside. "We can't get lost right here in the yard."

"You'd be surprised," Daniel said.

"A man and his family came to the dude ranch down the road for Christmas last year," Joshua said behind them as they trudged across what was supposed to be gravel, and was now a vast plain of snow. They couldn't even see the barn from here. "He thought he was heading for the big house from his cabin, and got turned around. They had to send out a search party."

"Did they find him?" Lovina asked.

"*Ja*, but it was touch and go. Someone had to take him in to the hospital in Eureka."

"How far is that?" Joel wanted to know.

"About ten miles. Impossible for a buggy. But it was the dude ranch, so they had a big dually truck with chains on the tires. Didn't take long at all, and he was back by suppertime, all thawed out."

Lovina peered through the flying snow as though wondering if they, too, might need a search party. Flakes were collecting on the wide knitted scarf she'd wrapped over her *Kapp* and around her throat and chin. "Joel, you are not to come back by yourself. You're to wait for Joshua to walk with you."

"But Mamm, I can just walk in our footprints."

"Your *mamm* is right," Joshua said, surprising Daniel. "Our footprints will be buried by lunchtime. We've lived here all our lives and know by instinct where things are. Best to stay with me until you know our place a little better."

Joel subsided, and Daniel met his brother's eyes with a nod. A word in season. In some places it could mean the difference between life and death.

The barn, when they finally made it through the big sliding doors, was warm and filled with the scents of hay and manure and the stamping and lowing of their few milk cows. Dat was already there, milking. He enjoyed it, and often as not would sing to the cows in his rumbly voice. Many a morning Daniel had done his chores to "*Wo ist Jesus, Mein Verlangen*," which had the same tune as the *Englisch* song "What a Friend We Have in Jesus."

Joel turned to his mother. "I can help Reuben milk, Mamm."

A chuckle sounded from behind the cow's broad back, over the music of milk hitting the pail. *"Neh,* Joel," Reuben said. "I am nearly finished, and you would not want to keep Joshua waiting for your help."

Joshua almost managed to keep from rolling his eyes as he waved the boy into the tack room. "See you at lunch."

Daniel hunted up the snow shovel and then ushered Lovina out the barn door into the swirling white.

"You're not going to start shoveling now, are you?" she asked as she picked her way back across the yard in the track they had made. Their deep footprints were already starting to fill. "There doesn't seem to be much point until this stops."

"Just the walks and the decks where we go in and out," he replied, doing his best to make a good trail for her to step in. "If I don't keep up with it, it will be all the more difficult to shovel when it finally does stop. One year Zach walked right off the front steps, they were buried so deep."

"Was he hurt?"

Daniel shook his head. "He wasn't very old. We just had to dig around him and he popped right out. But after that, we decided it was better to shovel off now and again rather than lose a sibling. And Dat put railings on the steps, too, just in case."

"Daniel Miller, I never know if you're telling me a tall tale or not."

"I'm not," he protested, but he couldn't help grinning at her mock severity. "Ask him."

"I noticed those railings last night. The wrought iron pickets with the wood rails are beautiful."

"A young blacksmith on the town side of the lake makes them. He does well with the tourists. Spends the winter smithing and the summers doing whatever ranch jobs he can get. Since our winters are a lot longer than our summers, he does all right."

"Does he shoe your horses?"

"He makes the shoes. But the farrier in Mountain Home—who is also our stock veterinarian—puts them on."

"He's the one who tended Cousin Joe's cow yesterday?"

"Ja. He's a busy man. Doesn't get too many days of rest around here. But he enjoys his work."

Of all the things he ever imagined talking about with Lovina, caring for stock wasn't one of them. Was she interested in his life here? Or just being polite to pass the time?

"What does your family do in the winter?"

"It's not winter yet. It's only the middle of October."

"Feels like winter." She tucked the end of her scarf into the collar of her coat.

"This will probably melt as fast as it came. Just a matter of getting through it until the sun comes out." They had reached the house, but she made no move to go in. Probably because the steps were nearly invisible. He got busy with the snow shovel. "When it's really winter, sometimes it doesn't snow for weeks. It's just bright and cold. Twenty, thirty below. By then the calves have been weaned and sent off to their buyers, and we do winter work."

"Fixing equipment and such? Like we do at home."

"*Ja*. With Amish folks, it's probably the same everywhere. Fixing machinery, keeping tack in good repair, making sure buggies are in good shape. We don't need Mamm or the girls breaking an axle or something on their way to town. We muck out the barns and the pens. Cut fence posts for spring. Cut firewood. Lots of firewood."

The shovel scraped on the fourth step and he

tossed the snow—the heavy, wet kind that fell when it was just above freezing—to the side.

"And then there's the cows. Who have to be fed. Every day."

"Like ours," she agreed. "They have winter forage, but when that gets buried, you have to take hay out, like Onkel Elmer used to do."

"*Ja.* We keep them fairly close in so we can reach them with the hay wagon. Some of the bigger spreads have pastures twenty miles apart. But they have tractors and trailers."

He'd shoveled his way up to the porch, where the deck roof kept the worst of the snow off until a person could get into the mud room.

"There you go," he said. "All clear."

"For now." She paused on the sisal doormat. "Are you never afraid, Daniel? Of all the things that could go wrong?"

What must it be like to live in fear like this? The perfect love of God was supposed to cast out fear.

But he didn't say that. Instead, he said, "If we prepare for the things that could go wrong, and do our best to avoid a problem, then we don't need to be afraid. *Der Herr* will look after the rest."

"But what if something unexpected happens?

Like a man getting lost in a blizzard, or the *boppli* falling off the stairs into the snow?"

"I'm pretty sure that's happened in Pennsylvania, too," he said slowly. "But the thing is, you do your best with what you know. You know who to call for help. Even the folks up at the dude ranch, worldly and hard to understand as they are, would be over here in minutes with their big truck if something really bad happened." He gazed at her, wondering if she feared for Joel this much in their everyday life. How could anyone live with a burden like that? "Life is sometimes a challenge here, Lovina, I won't deny it. But we help each other, Amish and *Englisch*. We depend on each other. And in the end, it helps make a good life. A rewarding life in the midst of the most beautiful country God ever made."

She turned as though to gaze out at the proof of what he said, but it was all curtained off by blowing snow. And in the end, she merely nodded, turned the doorknob, and went in.

Chapter 10

AT LUNCHTIME, Joel and Joshua came in to eat the mountain of sandwiches and bowls of hot soup that Naomi and her daughters had prepared. Being Monday, it was wash day, and Lovina had been hard at work with the mangle and then hanging the clothes on the lines that crisscrossed the basement, where the wood stove that appeared to heat most of the house would have them dry by tomorrow. Who had come up with the ingenious battery-powered heat pump system? Or did all the houses in this district have such a thing?

At supper, Joel told her all about the things he had learned. Lovina took note of the fact that the Miller men gently turned his occasional side trip into bragging back on to the main road of *demut* and learning, so skillfully that the boy never knew he was being disciplined not to draw attention to himself. Instead, he was encouraged to think of himself as part of a larger whole, each piece of which needed the others.

She was exhausted to the core by washing that would have to be continued tomorrow. How did Naomi keep up with five men's mud-covered clothes? And yet, the day was not finished. After supper, she went over Joel's geography lesson from his teacher. When the sheet was completed and Joel had brushed his teeth, said his prayers, and climbed into bed, she was an inch away from crawling into her own bed. But she must go down.

"You are schooling Joel as well?" Malena looked up from the jigsaw puzzle she was working on with her sister.

"*Neh*, not really." Lovina sat at the big pine table and took a chocolate chip cookie from the plate that always seemed to be there. "The Troyers' offer to take us with them came up so unexpectedly after the school year began that I was going to say no. But Joel's teacher thought that the education he would get from seeing the national parks would be so valuable that she encouraged me to go."

"Education in what way?" Rebecca asked. "Does it have something to do with the road map you needed earlier?"

"*Ja*. That was for geography. He was to map where all the parks are in the states drawn on that sheet. We have already mailed her our lists of animals we spotted in each park. The teacher wanted us to draw them, but I'm afraid neither of us is an artist. My elk look very much like his ground squirrels, and vice versa."

Malena giggled. "Zach is clever with a pencil. I bet he would give Joel drawing lessons." She raised her voice so her brother could hear her in the living room. "Wouldn't you, Zach?"

"I'm better at buildings than animals," he called back. "Unless Joel wants to draw an animal that looks like it was made of LEGO blocks."

"I'm sure that would be an improvement," Lovina joked.

"What else is he learning?" Rebecca asked.

"Let's see, we read the signs and learn spelling. We calculate the distance between towns on the highway signs for arithmetic, adding and subtracting as we go. And when we stopped at diners and eating places along the way, or at a motel for the night, I had him add up the price of meals or rooms, not only for us, but also for the whole party. Those got mailed away to his teacher, too."

"Including tax?" Daniel wanted to know from the depths of an easy chair, where he was reading *Western Horseman.*

"He won't have percentages until fifth grade," she said with a smile. "But by the time we got to Yellowstone, he could add up the cost of everyone's meals in his head."

"A handy skill," Reuben said, absorbed in the latest copy of the *Tägliches Manna.*

"Maybe I could help," Zach said thoughtfully. "I could draw a horse all tacked up and have him label all the parts of the tack. You know, like cantle and horn and headstall, all that. I guess I could do better than LEGO blocks for him."

"He knows the names of things well enough now," Joshua said. "I told him while we were cleaning each part."

"You did well," Reuben said, nodding. "The boy is teachable and smart."

Lovina glowed with pleasure—and so, she noticed, did Joshua. "How kind you all are to take notice of him and teach him."

"How else is a boy to learn?" Naomi gazed fondly at her sons over her knitting needles, which flashed in and out of the yarn so quickly Lovina could hardly follow them. She was knitting a sock, apparently to add to what seemed like the hundreds of socks Lovina had washed today. "We found with our boys that every day was like a classroom. Always something to learn."

"Only more interesting than a classroom," Adam said with a yawn. "Mamm, I'm going to turn in."

One by one they said good night and went up to bed, until at last Lovina realized she would be alone with Daniel if she didn't get a move on, too.

"*Guder nacht*," she said. "Maybe the snow will finally stop tonight."

"Are you in such a hurry to leave?" His gaze didn't leave the pages of the magazine, but it didn't look like he was reading it, either. And did he mean the ranch in general, or the living room, right now?

"I'm in a hurry to take the burden from your mother," she said carefully.

"Seems to me you did your share. Mamm told me you did the washing. You need to let the girls finish it tomorrow. You're our guest."

"I like to be busy," she admitted. "I don't want to sit at the table eating cookies while everyone around me is at work."

"You're giving Joel his lessons." Now he did put down the magazine.

In the lamplight, his hair took on rich chestnut highlights that it didn't have in the dull light of a cloudy day. His brown eyes under the two slashes of his eyebrows regarded her steadily.

With an effort, she dropped her gaze. "It doesn't take long. We have a worksheet for every day, but some days it's blank, so it's up to us how we fill it out. Like the cost of meals instead of a column of random numbers. If the snow does stop tonight, I'd like him to mail his worksheet tomorrow."

"It'll take a little while for the plows to get out here. Then Cathy, the mail carrier, will be able to get her truck in. Probably Wednesday. When it's cleared, maybe you'd like to learn to ski?"

Lovina blinked, the slow blink of surprise. What did that have to do with going to the mailbox? "I do not, *denki*. I have no desire to break my neck."

To her surprise, he laughed. "Not downhill skiing. That's more trouble than it's worth, and you have to pay for the privilege to boot. I mean cross-country skiing. It's pretty much the only way you're going to get down a quarter mile of lane to the mailbox until the snow melts. Unless you'd rather snowshoe. We can lend you a pair of those."

Her husband had used his snowshoes when the snow got particularly deep, but she'd never needed to go out into the fields that badly. "People ski on flat ground?" She'd never heard of such a thing.

"The more we travel the lane on foot or on skis, the more likely it is we can get to church on Sunday. Cross-country skiing is different. You might like it. You never go so fast that you hurt something when you fall." He thought for a moment. "Except maybe your pride."

Shaking her head, she wished him good night and climbed the stairs. Joel would love to ski to the mailbox to mail his worksheet to his teacher. He would see it as an adventure. Maybe she'd ask him to do a write-up of how he learned and what he saw along the way, for one of the open assignments. After all, Naomi had said that every day was a classroom.

But as she lay in the bed next to her son's, it wasn't a write-up about skiing to the mailbox that she struggled with.

She fell into an exhausted sleep doing her best not to think of the warmth of Daniel's eyes in the lamplight.

———

ON WEDNESDAY AT FIVE THIRTY, Lovina woke to Joel's excited news that one of the neighbors had telephoned. The snowplow had departed Mountain Home and the road would be cleared soon—maybe within the hour. At the window, while she couldn't see the plow, she could still see the stars, thicker and brighter even than in Pennsylvania. It must be the altitude and the dry air. They seemed enormous, the moon only the faintest sliver as it set behind the peaks.

It would be a clear day, and the Circle M would dig itself out.

She had learned in the last few days that after they said a silent grace, breakfast was always a noisy clatter completely different from the meals at Onkel Elmer's. Even with Mose, who was not much of a talker, her ingrained habit of silence made their meals a pretty sober event until Joel had come along. Then, they both had learned to laugh, and talk, and even teach. Mose had been a good father. A good husband. Not the husband she'd wanted, but the one she had chosen. At the time, that had been enough.

Lovina slid a glance at Daniel, who had thrown his head back in laughter at some silly joke between Zach and Malena. Never once in all the years she had been married had Mose laughed like that, with his whole being. He smiled, of course, and chuckled once in a while, but never laughed like this.

Shaken by the realization, she addressed herself once more to her bacon and eggs.

She needed to stop thinking about Daniel. As he'd said himself, the past didn't need to be dragged into the present to make things uncomfortable and even unseemly. He was content to be a *gut Freind*, and she should be, too.

So why couldn't she stop looking at him? At the way his hair curled on his forehead. The way his dark green shirt, modestly rolled down to the wrists, only showed how broad and strong his shoulders were. Honestly, what was the matter with the women in this district? How could they not see what an amazing husband and father he would be?

She reined in her thoughts before they ran away with her, and made herself useful washing the breakfast dishes. Reuben took Joel out to the barn, and she could see her boy whooping and jumping as he followed the trail they'd made yesterday. The sun would be up soon, the sky lightened now to a blue so bright it would hurt the eyes as the light bounced off the drifts of white.

The sun was fully up and warming the air when Joel returned. "Mamm, where is my worksheet from yesterday? Daniel says the mail will come before lunch. We're going to ski to the mailbox!"

She pulled an envelope and stamp out of their workbag and made him sit still long enough to address the envelope himself in careful capitals. Then he shoved it in the pocket of his coat. "Come on, Mamm!"

"Come where?" She pulled the knitted cap down over his ears. "I'm not going with you."

"But *ja*, you are. Daniel told me 'specially to ask you to come. Please, Mamm."

Behind her, putting away the dishes, Naomi laughed. "You'd better go, Lovina. You don't want Daniel marching in here to get you."

"Have *you* skied to the mailbox?" Lovina asked.

"*Ja*, sure. Many a time," she said, to Lovina's surprise. "One of the Wengerd boys' wives even skied to town once—two miles! But that was because she had to get medication for one of her *Kinner*, and her menfolk were up on the spring range when the blizzard hit. It was the talk of the town, but if it had been me, I'd have done the same."

Lovina believed it.

"Put on some heavy tights, and two pairs of socks. The skis are in the barn, along with the poles and the special shoes you wear."

She was in for it now. And if maybe she was guilty of a little pride that had her thinking that she could do it if Naomi could, well, she'd ask forgiveness for that later.

Joel was so excited that he could hardly stand still long enough for Daniel to fit him out with a pair of skis and the shoes that went with them, both clearly having belonged to the boys of the family when they were much younger. Lovina had never been skiing in her life, so it took her a few minutes to master the awkwardness of having slender lengths of fiberglass as tall as she was strapped to her feet. Once again her hair was hidden under a *Duchly* and hat, her hands warm in her gloves.

"Watch my stride," Daniel told the two of them. "You don't walk or run. You glide. Adam waxed the skis last night, so they won't stick. Let them help you travel over the snow, and stay in the tracks I make."

With that, he stamped awkwardly out of the

barn. But when he got into the snow, Lovina saw what he meant. He glided as easily as she used to skate on the frozen pond at Onkel Elmer's, borrowing her cousin's hockey skates until he found out and she was forbidden to do it anymore.

Joel clumped out into the snow and stepped carefully into Daniel's narrow tracks. Naturally athletic, he mimicked the gliding motion and in moments had crossed the yard. "Come on, Mamm! It's easy!" As Joel turned to say the words, he forgot he had skis on. His legs tangled and he tipped over in the snow like a sleeping cow.

Lovina tried not to laugh, honestly she did, but it happened so fast and with such perfect timing that she couldn't help it. By the time she had reached him, he was pushing himself to his feet and laughing, too.

"I guess the *gut Gott* has the last word about pride, Mamm," he said with a rueful grin. "I'll remember for next time."

By watching Daniel's movements and doing her best to let the skis help her in the way that skates did, Lovina followed in their twin tracks. They looked like a narrow-gauge railway the width of a person. And far faster than she could have covered the distance on foot, they arrived at the mailbox just in time to see a white pickup crest the hill.

The truck wallowed to a stop beside them. "Hullo, Daniel." The postal carrier rolled down her window and handed him a thick packet of mail. "Glad to see the plows are out all over Lincoln County."

"Morning, Cathy." He stamped sideways so that Joel could glide up and hand her his crumpled envelope. "This is Joel. He'll be sending his school lessons to his teacher back home for a couple of days."

"Is that right?" The blond, wind-blown woman looked about sixty, comfortable in her heated pickup. "Not from around these parts, are you?"

"We're from Whinburg Township, in Pennsylvania," Joel told her in his careful *Englisch*. "We got left behind so we're staying with the Millers until Cousin Joe can get us to the train or a bus."

Her eyebrows rose, but to her credit, she didn't ask any questions. "You'll have a fair wait, then. The train might be running, but there's no bus running out of Mountain Home until after the weekend, probably. Kalispell got it worse than we did, if you can believe it."

"Good to know," Daniel told her, even as the

bottom fell out of Lovina's stomach at the news. He slapped the sill of the door. "Drive safely."

"Shall do." Cathy put the truck in gear and headed down the road toward the Wengerd mailbox.

"Joel, why don't you go first this time?" Lovina suggested. "And be sure to observe what you see so that you can write it up."

When he was safely away and Daniel had tucked the mail into the big pockets of his coat, she preceded him down the track.

"I hope you're not worried about leaving," Daniel said. His skis made a singing sound behind her. "My folks don't mind a bit having the company."

"I should really go back to Cousin Joe's," she told him over her shoulder. "It isn't right when he is family."

"But as he says, there are more people here to keep Joel busy, and more women for company. Stop thinking of yourself as a burden, Lovina. We're happy to have the two of you. We'd be happy if there were six of you—we have a bunkhouse that's just as comfortable as the house, for when the hands hire on in the spring."

She pushed along the track they had made,

letting her body set a regular rhythm. "I can't help it. Maybe it's part of me now, this feeling."

"But why should it be?"

"My aunt and uncle—have I ever told you about them?"

"*Neh,* I don't think so."

Of all the things they had talked about on those sweet summer nights, her childhood had not been one of them. The teenage Lovina didn't want him to know she'd left them the year before, didn't want it to spoil the magic.

"My parents died when I was young, before they had a chance to have more children. I lived with several relatives all over Pennsylvania, until I finally got to Onkel Elmer and Aendi Grace's place in Smicksburg. Life was not easy for them there. They had six *Kinner* and never let me forget that I was another mouth to feed. I suppose I never have forgotten it, deep down."

Somehow, blurting it all out over a ski track seemed to take the sting out of it. It was only the past. Old news. And while it couldn't hurt her anymore, it had helped to form her character. To make her the kind of person she was.

He was silent for the space of six strides. "That's a sad way to make a child feel."

"*Ja,* I know that now I'm a parent myself. Back

then, it was just the way it was." She tried to make a joke. "Maybe that's why I'm so skinny. I never got in the habit of eating much, just to make sure they wouldn't send me somewhere else."

"Well, we're not going to send you somewhere else." His voice sounded a little gruff, but it could just be the cold air. It was warming, though. The edges of their track glistened, as though they were melting.

"But still, I—"

Joel shouted, and managed to lean on one pole and wave at something with the other without falling over.

Lovina looked across the brilliant expanse of acres of snow and cattle to see a lone figure, scarved and wearing a black coat like hers, skiing briskly inside the fence line next to the road. Skiing so smoothly and so fast that her green skirts belled out with the wind of her going. It was clear she'd had years of practice.

"Look, Mamm!" Joel shouted over his shoulder. "It's that Susan, the twins' friend. Look at her go!"

Chapter 11

SUSAN ANGLED across the pasture and met them at the feed gate, which Daniel had already opened for her. *"Guder mariye!"* she said gaily as she breezed through it. "I couldn't resist the snow, and it looks like you couldn't either."

Daniel closed the gate while Joel told her, "We went to the mailbox. Holy smokes, can you ever ski!"

"Joel," Lovina said. "Language."

"The boys at home say it," he said defensively.

"We do not swear by anything holy," she told him. "And nobody needs to swear by smoke."

He recovered from the rebuke and turned to Susan. "How did you learn to go that fast?"

"It took a little while." Susan's cheeks were red

and her nose was beginning to run, but she looked elated and robust. "A couple days of practice and you'll have it. But it's warming up. Half of this will be gone by tomorrow, I hope." She turned to Daniel. "Are the twins home?"

He stopped himself from asking where else they would be if the horses couldn't get the buggy down the lane. "*Ja,*" he said instead, and motioned for her and Joel to go ahead. "They'll be glad to see you."

"How about you?" she tossed over her shoulder as she stepped out in the track they had made.

"We all are," he said, but she was already moving.

He and Lovina fell into line behind her, and in a few minutes they had all reached the yard. While Susan took off her skis and stood them up next to the door before she went inside, the three of them followed their original track until it petered out at the barn.

"Better hurry," Lovina teased as Daniel exchanged the ski shoes for his work boots. "In case it isn't the twins she skied all this way to see."

Surely she couldn't believe he was interested in a girl who could be so forward? She was his sisters' best friend, and he was happy to keep her in what the *Englisch* called the friend zone. Better to let the remark pass. "Joel, let me help you with those fastenings," he said. "See, just take your pole and press on this clip here, at the back of your heel. Then you can step right out."

He tried not to be too obvious about taking his time getting them out of their gear, putting it away, and walking with them back to the house. He couldn't avoid the unavoidable, but he sure could put it off for as long as possible.

Malena and Rebecca must have finished the last of the washing, because they were in the kitchen talking a mile a minute with their friend. "You'll stay for lunch, won't you?" Malena said to her. "Then this afternoon you can help me plan my winter quilt."

"Sure, I'd love to," Susan replied.

Daniel resolved to make today the day he started on the fence posts, safely out in the woodshed.

"I can help, too," Lovina said. "I love to quilt."

Rebecca was setting the big table for lunch. "If Lovina can help you, then maybe Susan can help me with the mending. Daniel tore a big hole in his pants during roundup. It'll give her some practice."

The girls giggled, sounding like a spring creek

overrunning its banks, and Daniel escaped with Joel into the bathroom to wash up.

"I think that girl wants to go on a date with you," Joel informed him solemnly. "I don't think she came over here to see the twins at all."

"She's a *gut* friend to my sisters," he replied, handing Joel a towel. "She comes over all the time. But lucky for me, I get to choose who I ask out on a date."

"Who?" The boy's eyes held his, bright with curiosity.

If Joel was like any other child, whatever Daniel said would get back to his mother, probably within the hour, and probably in front of everyone. "I don't know. I asked a girl out once, but I guess she didn't like me as much as I liked her."

"Girls can say no?"

"Sure they can. And they should, if they don't like us back. They try not to hurt our feelings, but we get the message."

Joel thought this over. "But what if your *mamm* and *dat* like the girl and you don't?"

"Liking a person and inviting her to lunch is different from liking a girl and driving her home from Singing in your courting buggy or taking her by herself to get a hamburger in Mountain Home."

"There are hamburgers in Mountain Home?" Joel's mind jumped to this more interesting track, much to Daniel's relief.

"They're the best, except for Dat's barbecued hamburgers in the summer, with the special chile sauce that our Aendi Rachel in New Mexico makes. I'd pick those any day."

Joel pretended to pout. "I want to stay until summer and have one of Reuben's hamburgers."

Daniel laughed and tousled his hair. "When you turn sixteen maybe you can come on the train to work for the summer, and be one of our ranch hands."

"Truly?" Joel's eyes went wide with excitement. "I could work here?"

"Sure. You were a big help at roundup. I have a feeling ranch work might suit you."

"Like it suits you?"

Daniel nodded. "And now we'd better get to the table before someone thinks you're taking a bath instead of just washing your hands."

Giggling, Joel ran down the hall to the kitchen. Daniel followed at a leisurely pace. What must it be like to have a son like that? So interested in life around him, with a mind that wanted to absorb all it could. So openly loving, giving his friendship as though certain it would be returned. Had it been Lovina's training, or her husband's? Or a combination?

A picture flashed into his mind of Lovina and Joel at his own kitchen table, in their own home. They would be laughing, and Lovina would be expecting a child. Their child. A little *bruder* or *schweschder* for Joel.

"Daniel?"

The vision winked out like a candle flame, and he realized he was standing in the doorway with his family all staring at him.

"*Ja?*"

"Did you hear me?" his father asked patiently. "I said, who's been telling secrets about our chile sauce?"

"Not me," Daniel promised, taking his seat at the table. "I only told Joel that was why your burgers are so good, not what was in it."

After a silent grace, everyone dug into the elk-and-beef meatloaf with tomato sauce and the macaroni and cheese casserole.

"Susan's hamburgers are really good, too," Rebecca told them, passing the beet pickles to her friend. "What's in your sauce, Susan?"

"It's not the sauce, it's what I put in the hamburger patties themselves," the girl confided. "Crumbled goat cheese from our goats!"

"Eww." Joel's face screwed up in distaste.

"Joel!" Lovina chided him. "We don't criticize another's service to us, especially when Rebecca just said Susan's burgers *gschmeckt gut.*"

"To her, maybe," the boy grumbled. "Not to me, or to Daniel, I bet."

Daniel was staying out of this. And he privately resolved to give Susan's burgers a pass should they be on the menu when church was at their ranch next. Goat cheese had its place, but not inside a hamburger.

"I like goat cheese," Lovina said firmly. "How smart of you to think of it, Susan."

"It's from a cookbook," the girl said, modestly deflecting the compliment.

"Still, I heard Alden Stolzfus rave about them," Rebecca said. "That time we cooked out after the volleyball game."

"Alden Stolzfus would say the moon was made of cheese if he thought it would get a girl's attention," Malena said scornfully.

"Alden's a good guy who doesn't need a bag of tricks to get any girl to look at him," Zach told his sister. "His blacksmithing business is doing well and if you had any sense, you'd flutter your lashes at him."

Malena hooted at the idea. "I do not flutter my lashes!"

"Zachariah, stop teasing your sister," Naomi said, and passed him a plate loaded with thick slices of homemade bread. "Speaking of chile sauce, I got a letter in the mail today from your Aendi Rachel."

Malena explained to their guests, "Onkel Marlon died several years ago when a bull turned on him, so our aunt manages the Circle M spread there now."

"In New Mexico?" Lovina repeated. "I didn't realize there were churches there."

"There's a small district in the northern part of the state, in the Chama Valley," Naomi said. "Rachel's children are around the same age as ours. Three boys and a girl. The boys help their mother with the ranch work. Rachel wasn't sure how she would manage the business part of it in the beginning, but it turns out she has a knack for it."

"She ranches on her own?" Susan looked amazed. "I didn't realize she was a widow."

"My brother chose a good, capable woman," Reuben put in around a mouthful of meat loaf.

"Like you did." Naomi grinned at him.

He swallowed and gave a bark of laughter. "We Miller boys aren't stupid. We know a man's life is only as good as the woman he marries."

Naomi's smile hovered on her lips. "Anyway, Rachel says they're all well, and finished roundup last week, though minus all this snow. She's hoping your cousins will have a little time now to look around them."

"She means go courting," Rebecca confided to Susan. "Aendi Rachel is such a matchmaker."

"Nothing wrong with courting," Reuben said. "As long as the work gets done."

"Daniel needs to hurry up, or all the good ones around here will be gone," Adam said. "He might have to go to New Mexico and ask for *aendi*'s help."

"What about you?" Daniel retorted. Adam needed to keep his mouth shut. Susan already believed she was one of the "good ones," and she didn't need any more encouragement. "You could do with a nice, steady girl. What happened to that one you were writing to?"

Adam just shrugged. Either he didn't want to talk about it in front of the entire family, or the correspondence was over.

"Boys, this is hardly the time or place," Naomi

told them. "In my day, we kept our courtships to ourselves. Why, when your father proposed to me, that was the first my parents heard of it."

"But you were engaged for a year," Malena reminded her. "That was plenty of time for Mammi and Daadi to get to know him."

"And a good thing, too. We had to schedule the wedding—"

"Before spring calving," Daniel's siblings chorused. "Or there wouldn't have been a wedding at all."

Lovina laughed. "This sounds like a familiar story."

"We like a happy ending," Malena said. "Mamm grew up here, too. She knew what she was getting into."

Lovina fell into a thoughtful silence, and the conversation turned to other things. Then there were the dishes to do, and before anyone could make further remarks about torn pants and who was going to mend them, Daniel collected Joel and Joshua and escaped to the woodshed.

Chapter 12

DANIEL WAS NOT OFTEN glad for the shortening of the days in late autumn, but on the positive side, Susan only got to spend an hour with his sisters before the shadows began to lengthen and she was forced to ski home. He felt a profound sense of relief. After supper, when Lovina sat down with Joel at the table to compose his writeup of that morning's ski adventure to the mailbox, Daniel took himself downstairs to see to the wood stove before they all went to bed.

The new stove had gone in last year, and even Dat had to admit that saying farewell to the old faithful stove and installing the new one—complete with a window in the door and a catalytic converter in the top that made it much more efficient—had been a good use of hard-earned money. And when their *Englisch* neighbors had come over for dinner last winter, which was the only season when ranchers had time for socializing, invariably they walked in the door and said, "Oh, it's so nice and warm in here!"

Every ranch in the neighborhood had a secondary source of heat, for those weeks when the weather knocked out county power. But the Amish ranchers, being off the grid in the first place, knew the value of keeping a stove going and heating the house with it. Not for his parents the old custom of a stove in the kitchen and the doors open to the upstairs for heat to rise to the bedrooms. When Dat and the Meadowlark outfit built this house, they had put square grates in the floors above so that the heat would rise into the rooms unimpeded, and whether or not doors were closed. To help it up the basement staircase, a little fan sat on top of the stove, converting heat to electricity to run its motor.

Daniel had added wood and was waiting for it to catch before he closed the damper, when his mother came down the steps.

"Looking for a little peace and quiet?"

He smiled and lowered the damper's handle, then slid the air intake across so it was open only about an inch, to make it burn more slowly for the night and leave a good bed of coals that would ignite the fresh wood in the morning. "Two extra women at the table make a big difference."

"Not that Lovina is exactly a *Plappermaul*, but it was certainly lively."

"You just like the odds evened up a bit," he teased. "Five boys and five girls."

She laughed. "Maybe I do. But you seemed awfully quiet. I think you said more in the bathroom to Joel than you did to the whole group at lunch. And even less at supper. Is something going on with you, son?"

"*Neh, Mamm.* I'm all right."

She gazed at him, holding her hands out to the warmth of the stove. "Your sisters can be a little obvious about certain things. If that bothers you, I can have a talk with them."

"If *certain things* bothered me, I would talk with them myself."

"Well ... don't let the girls get carried away. Other people's feelings might be involved, and if you go along with it, you might be giving the wrong impression."

"I'm not giving any impression at all, as far as I know," he said soberly.

"Sometimes no answer can be read as a maybe."

Now he looked his mother in the eye. "What would you like me to do? I can't tell a woman no when she's never asked the question."

"It's not a woman's place to ask the question, *mei Hatz*. She's showing you she's interested. If you're not, don't keep her hanging."

"I'm not keeping anyone hanging. As I said, I'm not doing anything at all."

"That's about as useful as a horse not using its tail to flick off the fly. The fly is still there, still bothering the horse. Still hoping to get something."

He made a face. "I'm not sure Susan would appreciate being compared to a fly."

He thought this uncomfortable conversation might be over, but his mother merely turned to warm her back.

"You seem to take a good deal of notice of young Joel. It warms my heart to see it."

"I think we're all doing our part to make him feel welcome," he said cautiously. He had never told his parents about him and Lovina. There didn't seem to be any point. And now he was more thankful than ever for his tendency to keep things to himself. "With losing his father so recently, we all want to be good examples to him."

"He's a delight. Lovina is so good with him."

"*Ja.*" It was probably safe to agree with that much.

"Today's big bundle of mail held another letter," she said, in an odd tangent that wasn't like his orderly mother. "From Dat's cousin Melvin's wife, Carrie. Out there in Whinburg Township."

"Oh? They're well?"

"*Ja,* she's expecting a second child. Imagine that, after ten years barren, the minute they adopt their daughter, she gets pregnant. And now, barely a year after little Michael's birth, a second one on the way. *Gott* is surely *gut.*"

He nodded, wondering where this was going.

"She told me the goings-on in the township, and that Lovina and Joel were touring the national parks. Looks like the news of the van breakdown and their unexpected visit here hasn't reached her yet."

"So you'll tell her?"

"*Ja,* though it's likely the Troyers will beat a letter home. But she did tell me something else that was interesting."

He gazed at her, saying nothing.

"She was reminiscing, is all. Mentioned your

visit out there years ago. And wondered what might have gone wrong with that girl you were seeing." In the silence, they heard the muffled *pop* of wood behind the stove door. "You never told us you were seeing anyone that summer."

Daniel forced himself to speak past the gallop of his heartbeat. What had possessed their cousin Melvin's wife to bring that up now, of all times? "I didn't think it mattered. Nothing came of it."

"One of my boys getting interested in someone matters to me."

"It was only for a few weeks. And then I came home." He shrugged. "Not much to tell."

"What happened to the girl? Do you know?"

He tried to keep his voice even. Unconcerned. "She married someone else."

"An antique dealer, I understand."

"*Ja—*" he said, an instant before he realized he'd fallen right into her trap. "Mamm, don't—"

"Oh, I won't," she said, her own voice as even as his, but infused with the satisfaction of a detective who has solved a case. "I won't say a word. I just remember what your *Mammi* always used to say—*The hand of God is like the wind at your back. If you walk with it, you don't feel the cold.*"

Mammi had a proverb for every possible situation. As a child, he had puzzled over them many a time, and then had grown into understanding as he'd become older. "What is that supposed to mean?"

But she only smiled, and squeezed his arm. "You think about it."

And then she climbed the steps up to the kitchen, where he heard the approval in her voice as Joel showed her his work. No, more than approval. What he heard was the voice of a woman who couldn't wait to be a grandmother.

———

THE WEATHER WARMED to its normal October temperatures in the forties and fifties, much to the relief of the calves, Daniel suspected. And by Friday, the only reminders of the first freak storm of the season were a few humps of melting snow along the lane and on the north sides of the bigger trees.

His sisters had been clumsy amateurs in their efforts to make a match between him and their friend Susan. Their mother, however, was in an entirely different league. She was more than capable of arranging their lives in small ways that to him, were so obvious as to be embarrassing. She made Lovina feel so welcome and needed that even Daniel could see it would have been a wrench to suggest that now that the snow was gone, she might return to stay with her cousins. They had lives and young children of their own— most of whom were too young to play with Joel. Here, the boy always had something to do, whether it was taking riding lessons with Joshua or playing with the cattle dogs or cutting fence posts with Daniel.

As for Daniel, he gave himself a talking-to. The presence of a little boy he liked more and more each day was no excuse for shirking or even changing a day's work. Now that the snow was gone and the grazing was once more exposed, they had two weeks to wean the calves and get them in prime condition before they were delivered to market.

He invited Joel to man the gate between the two large fields they would use.

"I don't like weaning," the little boy confessed, bringing his smaller horse close to Daniel's as they and his brothers and father rode out. "I don't like it when the calves cry for their mothers. How come they have to be weaned?"

"So they won't get upset and sick when they're loaded on the trucks," Joshua said, riding easily beside him.

"Why do they do that?"

"Think how you would feel if you were here and your *mamm* was staying with Little Joe," Daniel said. "Wouldn't you feel lonely for her?"

"I guess," the boy said. "I wouldn't have to do my worksheets, though."

"Oh yes, you would," Reuben called over his shoulder. "We'd see to that."

"So the calves are lonely for their mothers and want to drink milk?"

"*Ja,*" Adam said from behind them. "That's why we use the fence-line method here. They can graze and drink and see their mothers, they just can't drink milk. We find that they wean in about a week as long as they think they're still together."

"And when they're calm, they spend less time roaming around trying to find their mothers and bawling," Zach said. "They eat more, so they weigh more, so they bring a better price."

"Do you have to sell them?" Joel asked. "I like calves. I like the one I caught even better."

"Can you tell which one he is?" Daniel asked, amused, as he dismounted to open the gate to the pairs' field.

"*Ja,* I can." Joel pointed. "That red one with the splash of white on his nose."

Half the cattle were red, mixed with black and

brown. Daniel could tell one calf from another if its behavior was unusual or it was sick, but that was about it. But then, it had been a while since he'd spent several hours with just one animal, as Joel had.

"We're going to cut the calves out and move them into the next field, there." Reuben pointed. "Joel, you go open that gate. Be sure you stand well to the side to keep it open, and don't block the entrance. The calves won't go in if they see you in their path."

Joel obeyed to the letter, and they spent the rest of the day cutting calves and moving them into the second field. The girls and Lovina brought sandwiches and coffee out to them to keep the process moving, and to his chagrin, Daniel found himself sitting straighter in the saddle and moving more efficiently at his task with Lovina watching. Marigold responded as though she knew what he was up to, wheeling and cutting and blocking the dams from following at the slightest touch of heel and knee. But their joint efforts were for nothing as far as Lovina was concerned—she was more interested in talking to Joel when he left his post and came over to eat.

"The calves aren't afraid of me," he told her

around his sandwich of thinly sliced elk steak and horseradish and lettuce. "But I'm glad Zach keeps the mother cows away. I don't think I want to get in the path of one of them when she's trying to get to her calf."

"I wouldn't like that either," she said with a shake of her head. "This mother is having a hard enough time seeing her baby in that field all by himself with all those calves." Daniel had to smile at her honesty even as Joel scrunched up his face.

"I'm not a baby," he said. "I'm a cowboy!"

But instead of laughing with the others, she looked stricken, the smile falling away.

The loss struck Daniel right through the heart. More than anything, he wanted to ask her what was wrong, why her son's doing his work well made her look as bleak as though he'd said he wanted to run away or leave church. But he couldn't say a word. The girls were packing up the lunch and Reuben's saddle creaked as he mounted up, which was the signal for them to get off the fence and do the same.

All he could do was watch Lovina walk away across the grassy field. When she caught his gaze, she made a point of looking away to where Joel was riding back to reopen the gate.

And then she joined his sisters and they were soon out of sight.

Working as a team, the "weaners" were all in their own field by midafternoon, and Reuben made Joel's face glow when he thanked him for doing his part so that Joshua could work another cutting horse. Daniel wondered how long it had been since the boy was included in men's work. Even if he was simply manning a gate, it was important and called for sense and good instincts if an animal made a break to rejoin its mother. Surely the men in the family back east had dairy cows, at least? Or did Lovina and Joel not live on a farm, but in town near the antique shop?

Daniel realized that for ten years, he had shut her from his mind so completely that he had not allowed himself this kind of curiosity about her life. And now that the floodgates had opened, he wanted to know the answers to a thousand questions.

Questions he might never ask, in case she told him that her life was none of his business. Which it wasn't. Because soon, she would be the one to leave—unless he found a way to change that.

Chapter 13

THE NEXT MORNING, Daniel came upstairs after stoking the fire in the basement stove, and accepted a cup of his mother's coffee gratefully. Zach and Adam liked theirs black, but he preferred his with a splash of cream, the way Mamm took it. The first sip of the morning was always the best.

"You make good coffee," he told his mother with a smile over the rim of the cup.

"Ach, you always say that," she said. "But what about your father's campfire coffee on a winter morning, up there on the mountain?"

Daniel laughed, and out of the corner of his eye, saw Lovina and Joel come in. "No matter how much cream or sugar I put in that brew, it's so thick and dark that it makes no difference at all."

Reuben's eyes crinkled over his own cup. "I make it that way on purpose, so you appreciate your Mamm's all the more."

"And I do, for sure and for certain," he agreed. "Still, I'd rather have yours up there than nothing at all."

"How did we miss out?" Lovina asked, pouring a glass of milk for Joel, then bringing her own cup to the table as the twins came in. "We had a cold morning on the mountain, and no coffee pot in sight."

"Poor preparation," Reuben said. "That'll teach me. Next time we get stranded, though, it'll be a different story. You'll see."

Daniel could practically see the *I will?* in her eyes.

"In the weeks before roundup," Reuben went on, "sometimes we're up there three and four days at a time, collecting cattle. A good strong pot of coffee is something to look forward to, and of course, Daniel manning the chuck wagon is always ... an experience."

Zach and Adam snickered.

"Hey," Daniel said in a wounded tone.

"Daniel makes the best biscuits," Adam said,

trying to keep his face straight. "Just ask the coyotes."

"Knocks 'em out on the first throw," Zach added.

Lovina laughed along with his family, and even though the joke was on him, Daniel grinned, too. He couldn't keep his eyes off her—laughter changed her usual calm demeanor to a sparkling, dimpled one that seemed to make the lamplight brighter and the room warmer.

Mamm and the twins served up breakfast, and after their silent grace, he poured maple syrup over his helping of casserole and swam a chunk of sausage through it. Joel took one look and did the same.

"This is *gut*," the boy said to Naomi, a beatific expression on his face. *"Was ischt?"*

"That is French toast casserole," she told him, lips twitching. "The secret is the cream cheese."

"I'm glad it's not goat cheese," Joel said.

Reuben cleared his throat as Lovina gave her son an elbow in the ribs. "Eat your eggs."

"After the sun comes up, I have a little job for you, Joel," Naomi said. "You might need your mother's help, though. And maybe even Daniel's."

"For what?" Joel abandoned the subject of goat cheese, and turned a puzzled face toward Daniel.

What was his mother up to? What job could a child do that might possibly need two adults along?

"I want the last of the apples out of Mammi's orchard," Naomi said. She was not looking at Daniel on purpose, it seemed to him. "It will mean taking the apple cart up into the canyon. That will hold six full bags, and you won't lose any of her good apples on the way down."

"But—" Rebecca began, when Joel interrupted.

"You have an orchard up in a canyon?" The boy had even stopped wolfing down the casserole at the strangeness of such an arrangement.

"My mother planted it there when she came here forty years ago," Reuben said, mopping up his own syrup with a chunk of fried sausage. "Our growing season is short in Montana – only a month in some places – so something like a fruit tree doesn't get much chance to produce. But she knew a trick or two, did my *mamm*. She planted half a dozen apple trees in a box canyon. It gets water all year round, and even when the days get shorter, since it faces straight south, it gets all the sunlight."

"And the walls of the canyon would shelter it from the wind and maybe some of the snow,"

Lovina said, nodding slowly. "That is a pretty smart trick."

"But don't the animals eat up all the apples?" Joel asked.

"Daadi built a fence around it," Malena said. "It keeps the deer and the coyotes out."

"Coyotes like apples?" Joel didn't look as though he believed it.

"They like anything that moves, and a lot of things that don't," Malena said. "Be careful up there."

"I want to see," Joel said. "We'll bring all the apples back safe, I promise."

He might not think it was such a good idea when he had to play the part of the horse and pull the cart up the trail, Daniel thought, but some things were best left for a man to discover for himself.

When everyone scattered to their chores after breakfast, Daniel took his mother aside. "What are you up to?" he asked in a low voice, while the twins and Lovina did the dishes.

"Why would you say that?" Her gaze was clear and guileless and it didn't fool him for a minute.

"The twins usually bring down the last of the apples for you. I've got things to do."

"That little boy has no father anymore to take

him out and teach him," Naomi said, and this time he knew she meant business. "You can take a morning to do that, and I'll hear no more about it."

"But—"

"The things you have to do will still be waiting for you tomorrow," she said with an air of finality. "A little boy may not be."

There was a truth he couldn't argue with. "All right," he said with a sigh. "I'll go dust off the cart."

———

AS IF TO MAKE UP FOR its unfriendly blizzard of a welcome, the Montana weather did another quick change as the sun rose into a cloudless blue sky. A warm breeze tugged on the strings of Lovina's *Kapp* as she climbed the path behind Daniel and Joel. Well, *warm* being relative. Her coat buttons were still done up, but she could imagine that when they got to the orchard, she could open them and maybe even take off the coat altogether.

Joel had bravely set himself against the apple cart's T-shaped whiffletree, designed for people, not mules or horses, and which hadn't fought him until the path began to wind up the side of the hill. "Do Malena and Rebecca really do this?" he panted halfway up, and staggered to a stop. "It's heavy."

"There are two of them, and they're bigger," Daniel said. "Want me to take a turn?"

Joel relinquished the cart, and they set off again. The air smelled of something vaguely familiar amid the dry grass and pines. "What's that scent?" Lovina asked. "I know it, but I can't place it."

"That's sage," Daniel said over his shoulder. "I bet you use it in the kitchen. It's everywhere around here, in the open places." He nodded toward the sinewy, silvery bush.

"With apples and sage, all we need is a Thanksgiving turkey, right, Mamm?" Joel walked ahead now, scouting the way.

"We might see a few of those," Daniel told him. "But we can't take a wild bird. It's deer season now, not turkey, and even on our own land, we have to obey the law."

Lovina couldn't remember the last time she'd walked just for the pleasure of enjoying God's creation. Perhaps it had even been with Daniel, all those years ago. Granted, it wasn't her pulling the cart, but it didn't seem to weigh on Daniel one bit.

They reached the box canyon a few minutes later and she realized that, even though it seemed they had been climbing a long time, they were still within sight of the house down in the valley. The beauty of the walk had made her forget both distance and time.

"Would you look at this," she breathed, setting her hands on her hips as Joel ran ahead to open the gate to the orchard for Daniel. The trees stood in two neat rows of three each, the lower branches bare of fruit from prior pickings, but still holding most of their leaves. The upper branches, however, still sported enough pale yellow fruit to fill their bags. The box canyon was more like twin outcrops of granite, with grasses and bushes growing all down their sides and a velvety mat of grass under the trees where nothing had been permitted to graze. "Will we leave some for the deer?" she asked.

"Yes," Daniel said with a smile. "The wormy ones."

Joel climbed nimbly into the first tree with a burlap sack. Daniel unhooked the short ladder from the side of the cart and leaned it against the next one. "What kind of apples are they, Daniel?" the boy called.

"I don't know what the root stock was—

Mammi never told me," he said. "But she had an apple man graft on these Lodi branches. Mamm likes them because they're good for pies and for drying both. Her schnitz pies are the best."

"My *mamm* makes good schnitz pie too. Can I taste one?"

"Sure. Toss the core over the fence and share it with the birds." He glanced over at Lovina. "Come on. I'll hold the ladder until you're comfortable."

"I have picked apples before," she told him dryly as she took a sack and climbed up. "We have Spartans and Delicious in our yard at home."

"Your husband farmed?"

"No, we live in town. We rent a little house, close enough so that I can walk to the shop. That meant a lot if Mose was away on a buying trip with our horse." She glanced down at him, her black skirts and kitchen apron belling out a little in the gentle breeze. "You can let go, you know. I'm not going to fall."

"I don't think I can." Before she could figure out what he meant, he straightened and released his grip on the ladder. "I guess this means I have to get to work, then."

"Be careful," she teased. "If you fell and broke a

leg, loading you on the cart for a fast trip down the trail would not be pretty."

He grinned and swung himself up into the sturdy branches of the tree as if he'd been doing it all his life. Which, she supposed, he had. Watching him not three yards away, his coat left on the cart and his shirt sleeves rolled up, was all kinds of distracting. And when his long brown fingers lifted each apple down with gentle efficiency it was all she could do to keep her own hands reaching for apples and not—

Oh, Lovina. He can still work that magic on you.

It had lain dormant for ten years and, as though it knew it had a short season, was doing its best to grow and bear its fruit now. She could remember completely losing her train of thought, back then, simply from watching him forking hay in the loft. Her mouth had gone dry at the sight of his wrists on his knees, his hands loose on the reins as they talked long into the evening on some back road. The way his mouth parted in a smile at the sight of her, that tiny dimple in the left corner giving her a perfect reason to kiss it. The way he—

"Mamm? What are you staring at?"

She came back to herself and looked down

through the reddening leaves to see Joel, the burlap sack bulging at his feet.

"I've got nearly a whole bag," he said proudly. "What did you see?"

"I was daydreaming," she confessed. "Well done, Joel. Put that one on the cart and take another bag."

"I'm going to pick two trees to your one, Mamm."

She wouldn't be surprised if he did. He ran down to the next tree in the row and scrambled up into the branches. In a moment his coat swooped down like a discarded skin and landed on the ground.

She finished picking a few minutes later, and descended the ladder with a full bag over her shoulder. Daniel jumped down and handed her a flawless golden apple.

"You should save the good ones for Naomi, so there will be a pie in your future," she said, and bit into it anyway. The juice exploded into her mouth and dribbled down her chin. "Mmmm, this is *gut*."

He sucked in a breath, and she swallowed the bite of apple with a gulp, as his gaze locked with hers. Like a man in a dream, he reached up and wiped the droplet of juice away. The touch of his finger, gentle as a feather landing, made her shiver.

She could no more control the yearning of her heart toward him than she could tell the breeze which way to blow. He was taller than she, and when she tilted her head back to look into his eyes, to see the truth she needed to see there, she fell up into that warm hazel gaze. How familiar it was, this sense of losing herself. Could it really be that the powerful emotions between them that had been torn in half might begin to knit themselves back together?

"Lovina-love," he whispered.

Crack! A branch broke, and someone screamed.

Lovina leaped away from him. "Joel!"

Her boy was hanging from an upper branch, apples strewn all over the ground beneath him, his feet kicking in the air as he tried to find purchase.

In the time it took her to get her feet moving, Daniel was already there, already vaulting into the lower branches and wrapping one arm around Joel's waist.

"It's all right," he said. "You can let go."

Joel slithered into his embrace and then Daniel swung him down next to the tree's sturdy trunk. By the time he had clambered to the ground, her boy was in tears.

"I'm sorry—I didn't mean to break the branch —I slipped—"

Lovina took his hands to examine them for cuts. "It's all right, Joel," she said in as soothing a tone as her galloping heart would allow. "You have a little cut here, and a big scrape here, but we'll get you home and put good old Burn and Wound on it. By tomorrow you'll be good as new."

"But the apples," he wailed. "I dropped the bag and they're all ruined."

"You're more important than apples," Daniel said, already gathering them into the bag. "Mamm will make apple crisp with the bruised ones and no one will know but the three of us. Dat will just thank her for making his favorite dessert."

Joel sniffled and closed his cut hand protectively. It had already stopped bleeding. "He will?"

"She's made plenty for just that reason," he said with a smile. "You might ask Joshua sometime about the day he let the loaded cart get away from him on the way down the hill."

"*Neh.*" Joel's eyes widened.

"*Ja.*" Daniel handed him his burlap sack. "We

were finding apples in the strangest places for months. Mamm even found a little seedling trying to grow in her garden, two years later."

Lovina could see that Joshua's disastrous experience was putting his own well into perspective. After all, nothing could be worse than losing a whole cart loaded with apples—and in front of your brothers, to boot.

"Come, *mei sohn*," she said. "We'll pick the rest another day. We need to wash that cut and get ointment on it."

Daniel lifted Joel on to the cart with instructions to brace himself against the front wall and use their coats to make sure the bags didn't jostle too much and bruise the fruit any further. He didn't have to do that, Lovina thought. But wasn't it just like him to make a little boy forget his hurts in a new adventure, learning to be useful even while he was getting a ride down the hill.

And wasn't it just like her to love him for it.

Lovina drew a long breath. Her feet forgot to move while her mind caught up to what her heart already knew.

She loved him. She always had. Always would.

And even if he never spoke—never touched her again with the kind of tenderness he'd shown a few minutes ago—she would carry him in her heart forever, like a warm flame.

Daniel looked back, the cart already bumping along behind him. "Lovina?"

"Ja, ich komme."

She would follow him wherever he led, if only he would ask her to. But maybe he would not ask. Had she hurt him so badly in the past that he could no longer trust her with his future?

Chapter 14

SUNDAY MORNING, Lovina and Joel were early risers in order to help the Miller family get breakfast on the table and get the buggies ready to go to worship.

Today's service would revolve around the third chapter of John and the sixth chapter of Romans, the word of the Lord on the subject of new birth. Since the service two weeks from now would include Council Meeting, and the one after that would be Communion, it was tradition that, in the weeks before taking the body and blood of Christ, the *Gmee* would cleanse themselves in spirit in order to be as ready as an imperfect human being could be.

"One of the ways to cleanse the soul before

Communion," Lovina said to Joel as they made their beds, "is to ask forgiveness of anyone we have wronged. Even if we haven't joined church yet, it's good practice for when we do."

"Everyone?" From the look on her boy's face, his list had far too many people on it to count.

She tried not to laugh, though in the lamplight she was certain he would be able to see her dancing eyes. "Everyone we can."

"But what kinds of wrongs, Mamm?" They went down the stairs together and into the kitchen, where Naomi was just taking a tray of pecan and maple buns out of the oven.

"Well, if a young man had an argument with his best friend, for instance, he would make it up before he took communion. Ain't so, Naomi?" She appealed to the experienced mother of six.

"*Ja.*" Naomi took off her oven mitts as the rich scent of maple syrup filled the kitchen. "Or if one of the boys had backtalked their father and hadn't asked forgiveness, now would be a good time to do it. Or if Reuben had promised someone something and forgotten to do it, he would make sure that thing got done before Communion."

"We must all learn to ask forgiveness no matter how old we are," Lovina told him, and Naomi nodded briskly to back her up.

"Adam and Joshua have joined church, but we haven't yet," Malena said from the stove, where she was frying eggs. "We still make sure and certain we have nothing bad in our hearts to take forward into a new year."

"Oh." Joel's brow furrowed as the men came into the mud room from milking, pulling off boots and shrugging out of their coats. "I don't think I have anything bad in my heart. Except for calling Elijah Peachy a dunderhead when he made me lose that trout in the summer."

"Did you say you were sorry?" Lovina asked.

"*Neh.* He got his line all tangled up with mine and I had to cut it. And I had a really big fish!"

"Are you sorry now?" she persisted.

Joel looked thoughtful. "I s'pose. He didn't mean to get tangled up. He was pretty excited. It was the *Grossdaadi* fish."

"Then maybe sometime this week you might write him a letter," Rebecca suggested, offering him a crispy potato slice from the big cast-iron frying pan. "He might still feel bad that you called him a name, and your letter might make him happy that you're still friends."

"He knows we're friends," Joel objected, crunching up the potato with relish. "I shared my sandwich with him at school the very next day. Everybody saw us."

"But he might not know you're sorry about calling him a dunderhead," Lovina said gently. "Because only God knows that. And now, us."

Joel cocked his head. "Who are you going to say sorry to, Mamm?"

"Maybe I've got some letters to write, too. Maybe more than one."

"But who to?" He looked as though he couldn't quite believe it, but since it was his mother admitting the fault, it was mighty interesting.

But now the men were all coming in and crowding the big utility sink to wash their hands, and personal matters had to be set aside.

After that moment of revelation in the apple orchard, a conviction had been born in Lovina's heart that it was time for her to be honest with herself, and with Daniel. Granted, he didn't seem very interested in hearing her reasons for turning down his proposal all those years ago. But he had listened, at least, when she'd attempted to tell him a little about her childhood. Maybe, if she could find a time and a place, she could tell him a little more. And eventually, get to the place where she could ask his forgiveness for hurting him.

And then ...? She did not know what his feelings were toward her. She might leave here still not knowing. But she knew her own feelings now. The rest was in God's hands.

As she took her seat at the big, noisy kitchen table, and afterward as the women cleaned up and got ready to leave for worship, she saw that she must have hurt him far more than she'd ever realized. There must be many reasons why a man of twenty-eight—kind, handsome, hard-working and talented—had not yet married. But could one of those reasons stem from that starry night on the bridge over Willow Creek?

Surely it was prideful to think that she could have had anything to do with his choices in life. But what if it were true? Perhaps this was why the *gut Gott* had brought her so far across the country at this particular time—to see Daniel Miller as he was now. And to ask his forgiveness. They might both take communion with hearts cleansed of that old hurt, and maybe, just maybe, begin again.

She pondered it during worship, sitting next to Naomi and doing her best not to crane her neck to check on Joel, who was sitting with the Miller men and looking as pleased as could be about it. He had gone with them almost naturally, filing onto the bench and sitting between Reuben and Daniel, though by rights he should still be with her. With a pang, she realized it was yet another step he would take away from her. Soon he, too, would take his seat just before the first hymn with all the young, unmarried men, as Zach, Adam, and Joshua were doing. And then he would be courting, and married, and ...

She sighed. It was God's plan for His children. And yet her heart cracked a little at the thought.

The service began at eight and ended at eleven-thirty, just as it did at home. The *Loblied* was the second hymn, just as it was at home. The *Gmee* in this district were not large in number; the King living room held the fifty or so people comfortably, with only a few sitting in the kitchen. She knew that Cousin Joe also had the responsibility for a very small district a few miles up the road, where he alternated with his own every other week. After the service, when the men had broken down the benches and set up the tables for the communal meal, she joined the women in setting out the food—bread, soup, peanut butter spread for the young ones, and all kinds of cold meats, cheeses and pickles, pies, and cake.

It was so much like home that she almost began to wonder what her idea of Montana had been all those years ago. A howling wilderness? A place where bears and avalanches and numerous other dangers just waited to spring out at the unwary like herself? She was coming to see that a person didn't just strike out into the wilderness unprepared, because of course it would strike back. Everyone she had seen so far respected the mountains and forests around them, even partnering with them, as they did when they grazed the cattle in the high country. Naomi had told her, laughing, it was just as much an adventure taking them up in the spring as it was bringing them back again in the autumn, only with more mud.

And listening to her neighbors talk, joining in occasionally, she realized that every one of the people here at the table loved this corner of Montana. The oldest member of the congregation, who had been introduced as Annie Gingerich and was ninety-six, was regaling them in her cracked, wavery voice with the story of her first winter in the original settlement at Rexford, the winter they'd had ten feet of snow and had to climb out through the second-floor bedroom windows to do the milking.

And yet they had done it, with God's help, and determination, and even humor. It must have been frightening. But today, it made a good story, one that it seemed everyone had heard, but never tired of. It brought the congregation together in a way that Lovina had never seen before, in a common experience of the trials of land and weather. There were plenty of trials in Whinburg Township, too, but there were also many more people there to help. A hospital close by. A *Dokterfraa*. And no bears.

It took a certain kind of person, she was coming to learn, to trust God enough to be a light in this place, if He had made it clear He wanted that person here. No wonder Daniel hadn't been willing to make his home in Pennsylvania. He had been called to this life, this place, and he had acted in obedience to that call.

Maybe she had more to ask forgiveness for than she thought.

After lunch, the weather warmed up to the point that people could stroll in the yard with their coats unfastened. Joel was in the orchard, playing tag among fallen leaves under the trees with the other boys. These were the first Amish boys his age he had met since their unexpected visit had begun. He had lots of friends in Whinburg Township, because he was a social little boy, but he'd grown up with them all. Making new friends with experiences different from his own was new to him.

Cousin Joe joined her as she gazed out over the garden, completely finished now, turned under, and very likely sown in radishes that would be turned under again to provide nutrition to the soil for the next planting.

"Off by yourself?" he asked, the boom of his voice lowered practically to a whisper, his magnificent beard as white as fresh snow, though he was barely sixty yet.

"Watching Joel," Lovina said with a smile, and a nod toward the boys, who had now run to the fence to talk to the buggy horses. "He makes friends so easily, like his father did."

"And you? Do you find it easy?"

"Not as easy as he does. During those years with Aendi Grace and Onkel Elmer, it was difficult to make friends when I thought I might be bundled into a buggy tomorrow to go to someone else's house."

"Ach, that must have been hard. Onkel Elmer is a *gut* man, but he's better with dairy cows than with children."

She nodded. "He does love his cows. I learned not to feel sorry for myself. I learned to be useful, and to find a safe place where I could go when I felt lonely. I fed a lot of barn cats, bribing them to be my friends." She chuckled, watching a horse investigate one of the boys' pockets from behind.

"I hope you know you have friends here," Cousin Joe said, as the boy realized he was being pickpocketed and dug a carrot stub out of his pocket for the horse. "As for me and mine, and I know for the Millers, too, we are happy to have you stay. You don't need to be in a hurry to catch that train."

"*Denki* for saying so, but I still don't feel quite right about taking a bed in the Miller house when it's you who are family. They've told me more than once that I'm as welcome as a sister, and that it's *gut* for Joel to have the *Youngie* to teach him and play games with him. But I can't think of a better model than you."

The bishop rocked up on his toes and back, chewing on his upper lip.

"Joe?" she said. "What is it?" Had she embarrassed him?

"My wife, my daughter, and my daughters-in-law will all haul me out to the woodshed for this," he muttered.

Lovina had to laugh. "I hardly think Sadie leads *you* around by the nose. For one thing, she can't reach it, can she?"

Now he laughed, too, for his height was the reason for his nickname. "Ach, I'm halfway to the woodshed as it is, for eating some of the pie she had planned to bring today. I may as well tell you."

Lovina didn't know whether to be amused or worried.

"It seems my womenfolk are trying their hands at a little matchmaking."

She tried not to show her dismay. "So are the Miller girls. If Daniel isn't engaged to Susan Bontrager by Christmas, it won't be for lack of trying." She kept her voice light, conversational. "You must know her as well as anyone. Do you think she will make a *gut Fraa* for him?"

"Susan Bontrager?" her cousin repeated, his brows rising under the brim of his black hat.

The horses took alarm at something and galloped away, leaving the boys to climb the fence, fruitlessly calling them back.

"*Ja,*" Lovina said. "Talk about the woodshed— Daniel had to go hide in there the other day, just to get a moment's peace."

"His sisters are trying to match him up with Susan?"

"Is that what Sadie is up to, as well?"

His laugh boomed out, and several of the

Gmee turned to look, smiles breaking out on their faces as though it was a familiar and welcome sound. "I think you are right, Lovina. I will be making an announcement in church by Christmas. But I very much doubt the happy bride will be Susan."

Laughing, he walked away to circulate among his flock, leaving her mystified.

Chapter 15

WAS it always like this for Daniel—his neighbors trying to match him with this young woman and that one? And how might someone like Susan Bontrager feel, who had known him all her life? But in her case, you'd think that if something were going to happen, it would have happened long before now.

For Lovina, it had happened in an instant. She had been down on the path next to Willow Creek, picking flowers to put on the dinner table at her cousin's, where she was staying after leaving her aunt and uncle's farm, when something had made her look up. There he'd been, the new boy, leaning on the rail of the bridge and smiling down at her.

That smile had brought something new into her unhappy life.

"Guder owed," he'd said. "It's Lovina Wengerd, isn't it?"

"Ja." One hand full of flowers, she'd shaded her eyes against the sun to get a better look at him.

"I'm Daniel Miller. I'm helping at our cousin Melvin Miller's place this summer. We met at singing on Friday. But maybe you don't remember? Wouldn't blame you if you didn't."

Did she remember. And had spent most of that night dreaming of his handsome face and his kind hazel eyes, to the point that she'd slept in until nearly six and had been teased unmercifully by her cousin.

He crossed the bridge to her side of the creek and scrambled down the bank, where they'd spent the afternoon talking and laughing and forgetting about the flowers, which meant she'd had to hastily pick a whole new bouquet and hurry back to her aunt. The next Friday, he'd asked if he might take her home in his borrowed vehicle, which was the Miller pickup wagon because Melvin and Carrie had taken the *Kinner* in the buggy to supper at Emma and Grant Weaver's. But she hadn't cared that it wasn't a smart new courting buggy, or one with fancy reflectors on the back and a battery-powered stereo system under the seat. She would have gone home on the back of a push scooter, as long as he was the one steering.

It was not lost on her that he had proposed on that same bridge where they'd first met on that summer afternoon. Only by then it was the beginning of September, and the scholars were going back to the classroom and he was going back to Montana to be there in time for roundup.

He had gone back alone, and had not come back. And here they were.

She caught sight of Anna Wengerd, Joe's daughter-in-law, heading toward the family buggy, so she hurried over to talk to her in case they were getting ready to go home.

"Hallo, Lovina," she greeted her. "I've hardly had a chance to visit with you since you've been here. How are they treating you over at Millers'?"

"Like family," Lovina said frankly. She liked Peter's wife, whose eyes had not lost their sparkle despite her growing family, nor her mouth its dimples. "But I still think I should be with Sadie and Ruby. The house must be so big with all the other *Kinner* married and gone."

Anna laughed at the idea. "We're over there half the time anyway. I think Mamm is glad to have some quiet to read her books, and Ruby the time to work on her quilts. She sells them in the quilt shop in Mountain Home, you know. The *Englisch* tourists have discovered us, and there's quite a good demand."

"Who owns the quilt shop?" Lovina asked. "Malena was talking about it the other day, hoping that she could take one or two of hers in to sell on consignment. She's a beautiful quilter."

Anna turned to look over the knots of people. "I don't see her—she must be inside. But the owner's name is Rose Stolzfus. She's fairly new to our community—she and her *Kinner* came about ten years ago."

"That's new?" Lovina said in amusement.

Anna tilted her head to acknowledge the point. "Her oldest son is Alden, the blacksmith. He's the tall one in the dark blue shirt, over there by Malena and Adam and the others."

Alden might have been called skinny if it hadn't been for the broad shoulders and capable hands that demonstrated his line of work. Lovina saw that while Malena was chattering away to her circle of friends, Alden stood a few feet apart where he had a good view of her face.

"Is he sweet on Malena?"

Anna took more interest in the little group. "What makes you say that?"

But he had turned to talk to Adam, and the moment was gone.

"Your *dat* says you and your sister-in-law might have an idea about Susan Bontrager and Daniel Miller," Lovina said, doing her best to sound as though she were teasing.

Anna looked startled. "Dat said that?"

"*Ja*, and he said he was headed for the wood-shed if it got out, so my lips are sealed." She pretended to turn a lock on her lips and throw the key over her shoulder.

"What do you think of our ... idea?" Anna said, watching her. "Is it a *gut* one?"

"I think poor Daniel ought to be left to work things out his own way," Lovina said with her best impression of a laugh. "The surest way to scare a man off is for him to find out the women are ganging up on him."

"But Susan Bontrager," Anna said, as though she was the last woman anyone could consider for Daniel.

"Don't you like her?" Lovina asked curiously.

"Oh, everyone likes her. I just don't know if she's the girl for Daniel."

Now Lovina was confused. "But your father told me you and Katherine both thought she was."

Anna turned to look over the buggies behind them, as if she were trying to locate hers. "In the end, it's not what we think. It's what *der Herr* thinks, ain't so? You'll have to excuse me, Lovina. I need to round up my *Kinner* and my husband and head home. It's nearly three o'clock." Then she touched Lovina's hand. "You should come to Sisters' Day with us on Tuesday. It's at my mother-in-law's, at one o'clock. We're making a wedding quilt."

"Oh, I'd love to. For whom?"

But with a twinkling smile, Anna hurried off, leaving Lovina to wonder if she'd put her foot in it as far as poor Susan was concerned. Which was downright *batzich*, considering she didn't want Susan to need that wedding quilt at all.

And wasn't she just the dog in the proverbial manger?

———

IT HAD BEEN a long time since Daniel had felt the urge to take a Sunday drive and go with the *Youngie* to someone's house for singing. Today was no exception, especially with Susan heading straight for him like a woman on a mission. He made a show of checking Cody's harness, only turning when she greeted him.

"Hallo, Daniel. Did you hear that singing is at Alden Stolzfus's house? Are you coming?"

"*Ja,* I did hear, and *neh,* I wasn't thinking of it."

"That's a shame." All the smiles faded from her face. "It would sure be nice if you came. Zach and Adam are. But we haven't seen you out in ages."

"I came once," he said. "In the summer. But it's not easy to get away."

"No one knows that better than I," she said. "There's always something that needs to be done on a ranch, isn't there? But it's Sunday. A day of rest and fellowship."

"We've been blessed with fellowship today," he agreed blandly. "It's good to be content with what we have."

Without warning, Joel Lapp popped out from between the buggies with little Thomas Wengerd at his heels. "Daniel, Mamm says can we get a ride back to the Circle M with you and Adam and Zach?"

Daniel stopped fiddling with a leather strap in his surprise. "What happened to Mamm and Dat?"

"I dunno." Joel shrugged. "I think they're going to supper somewhere."

This was odd. "Then I'd better talk to your *mamm*. I hear Adam and Zach aren't coming back with me, so I think someone might have got their lines crossed somewhere."

Susan laughed. "See? You should have come with us. Why don't you come after you finish playing taxi?"

Susan had a reputation for bluntness, but this was taking it too far. She made it sound like Lovina and Joel were suitcases he had to leave on the porch before he could get on with his evening. But all he said was, "We'll see."

He managed to lose her among the departing *Gmee*, and saw Lovina coming down the front steps of the house with the tote bag Mamm used to bring her contribution to the lunch. She had her away bonnet on, and her handbag over her shoulder. A sure sign a woman was about to leave.

"Did Joel find you?" she asked with a smile as she joined him.

"He did, but I think there's some confusion."

"Oh? Naomi and Reuben are staying here for supper and a visit, and the twins, Zach, and Adam are going to the singing. That's not so confusing."

"They all got rides?" The logistics of only having two buggies could sometimes defeat them on a Sunday like this. "It's high time Zach spent some of his savings on a buggy for himself. That way they could all go together."

She laughed at the idea. "That wouldn't make Alden Stolzfus very happy. I understand he convinced Malena to go with him and Rebecca isn't over the shock of it yet."

Rebecca, always the quieter one, the one less noticed, would feel better when the shoe was on the other foot, if that day ever came. "So that leaves us ... where? With Joshua?"

"He's gone," Joel piped in. "I saw him walking down the road right after lunch."

"Of course he's gone." Daniel shook his head. "All right, then, it's just the three of us."

Just the three of them, like a dream, only he was still awake. For a couple of miles, he could pretend they were a family going home. Just him and Lovina and the thousand things he wanted to say, but couldn't because Joel was sitting between them on the bench.

"I remember leaving church in your buggy and the awful teasing we got when we arrived at the house where singing was," Lovina said softly as he shook the reins over Cody's back and they trotted out on the main road. "It's one thing to ask a girl if you can give her a ride home afterward, when it's dark. But broad daylight seems different. No secrets there. A girl can't even wait at the end of the driveway to scramble into the buggy—everyone can still see her."

Daniel chuckled. "Think they'll be talking about us?"

"I hope not," she replied with a smile. "Though I suppose to make it completely gossip-free, I could have gone home with one of my cousins. The bishop and Sadie just left, too."

"I'm glad you didn't," came out of his mouth when what he'd meant to say was, "It's more practical that you didn't."

"I'm glad, too," she said softly. "My Aendi Grace was consumed with what people would say about every move we made. I'm not saying we should do what we want without thinking of God first, and other people next. But at the same time, being ruled by what other people think seems like it would suck the joy out of life." She glanced at him and her eyes held a warmth he hadn't seen in a long time. "Today, I decided to be happy instead of sensible."

"Do you do that often?" he managed, hardly

able to breathe. Was she saying that being with him made her happy?

"This is the first time in a while," she confessed, her gaze on the splendid view of the mountains in the distance. "It's probably been a good ten years since..." Her voice trailed away, as though she realized she might have revealed too much.

But from the lightness in his heart, you'd think she'd confessed far more than that. If only he could—

"Daniel, can I drive?" Joel said eagerly. "As soon as we turn in at the gate?"

And in handing over the reins and watching Cody so he didn't take advantage of an inexperienced touch, the opportunity to reply was lost.

But this lightness inside him, this spark of happiness, didn't go away.

In fact, throughout a homey, quiet evening in which she made a pick-up supper and then the three of them worked on the twins' puzzle, it seemed as though the feeling only increased. It was like the lights of home, growing brighter the closer you came.

———

MONDAY EVENING FOUND Lovina and Joel struggling with the intricacies of multiplication. His scratch paper was covered in increasingly sloppy columns of numbers, and she knew a bout of frustrated tears might be imminent. Then she had a brain wave. Why not make the numbers real to him?

"Joel," she said thoughtfully, "if you had three calves in the weaning field and multiplied them by two, how many would you have?"

Her son squinted into the distance, as though he saw them. "We call them weaners, Mamm."

She smothered a smile. "*Ja*, all right. Three weaners."

"I'd have six."

"And if you multiplied the six in the field by eight?"

"A couple dozen."

"Specifically."

He thought for a moment. "Forty-eight? That's a lot of weaners."

"*Ja*, it is. So write that down on your work-sheet before we forget."

He did so as Daniel came to lean on the door frame to the living room. "And how many legs do the original six weaners have?"

Joel looked up in surprise. "Legs?"

"*Ja.* Six calves have how many legs in total?"

"Twenty-four!" he said triumphantly, and wrote the equation down.

"Now, how many horns will they have when they grow up?"

"Depends how many males you've got among them six," Reuben said from behind *The Budget.*

"They're all males," Daniel said, nodding. "Keep it simple."

"Twelve!" Joel crowed. Another equation accomplished.

"Now," said Lovina, "if instead of multiplying, we just added eight weaners to the field and then Adam and Zach cut them into two equal groups for feeding, how many would be in each group?"

This was a stumper. Joel wrote the first equation carefully, then raced to the answer of the second. "Seven!"

"Well done." Rebecca's voice was filled with approval as she looked up from the jigsaw puzzle. "That was a hard one."

Then Adam threw out another hard one, and Joshua, laughing, gave her boy a third. Joel had a little trouble with Zach's, but with Daniel giving him a hint, he got the answer, and their worksheet with its twenty required problems was soon done.

"Arithmetic always makes me hungry," Naomi said as she set aside her knitting and came into the kitchen. "Who's for cherry pie?"

As Joel scrambled off his chair at the big table to help carry pie and ice cream to everyone, Lovina wondered how on earth she was ever going to separate him from this family. For the fact hanging over her head was that he needed to be back in school. The worksheets and writing assignments were only meant to be a stop-gap while they were touring the national parks with the Troyers. They were no real substitute for Hannah, his teacher, and the companionship of the other Willow Creek scholars learning and helping each other along.

Much as it hurt to think about it, much as she would give anything to be able to put it off, she could no longer afford to indulge either herself or Joel.

"I wonder if I might borrow the buggy tomorrow?" she said to Naomi, who had led them into the living room with their pie. Lovina settled into the chair next to her and took a gooey bite. Sublime. She swallowed and went on, "Peter Wengerd's Anna invited me to Sisters' Day at the bishop's home at one o'clock, but I thought I might go into town before that and use the library Internet to look at the train schedule."

Naomi put down her fork. "You don't need to feel in any hurry to leave, Lovina."

"I know. Bishop Joe said that, too. And I'm so grateful for your kindness." She dropped her gaze to her melting ice cream. "But Joel needs to be back in school. Now that the roads are dry, I wouldn't be dealing honestly with his teacher if I extended our holiday any further. We were only supposed to be gone three weeks, and it's been nearly five."

"Mamm," Joel complained.

Reuben put a hand on his knee. "Your mother is right. It would not be honest." To Lovina, he said, "Do you know your way to town?"

"If I turn right at the end of the lane, it's a couple of miles to Mountain Home?"

Reuben smiled. "Both the library and the train station are in Libby, five miles farther on. Maybe one of us should go with you, and you can drop whoever it is back at the gate on your way to the bishop's."

"I'll go," Malena said. "I want to talk to Rose in the quilt shop."

"No, I'll go," Joshua told her. "Could be I'll run

into some friends and Lovina won't have to trouble herself with bringing me back."

"You'll be checking calves with Adam and Zach," Reuben told him firmly. "And taking young Joel out to the fields to show him what to do."

Joshua's face took on a stormy expression. "Daniel can do that. He's good at being the boss of other people."

"I'm going with Lovina," Daniel said quietly, ending what was about to become an argument. "We'll just get the information from the horse's mouth, at the station."

"But I can—" Malena began, only to be silenced by a shake of her mother's head.

"*Denki*, Daniel," Lovina managed to say in a relatively even tone. "That's very kind of you. But surely the cattle need you more."

"I don't see why I can't go." Malena's brows wrinkled together and for a moment Lovina saw the resemblance between her and Joshua. "I know where everything is."

"What day is it tomorrow, Malena?" Daniel asked her.

"It's Tuesday the twentieth, which you would know if you looked at the wall calendar *right* behind you," his sister informed him.

"And what day is that?" Daniel persisted.

"Good grief, how should I know? It's not your birthday." She shoveled a forkful of pie into her mouth as if, Lovina thought, she wanted to stop herself from venting her annoyance.

Adam snapped his fingers. "It's opening day."

"Oh my goodness, of course," Naomi said, rolling her eyes in a *how could I have forgotten?* kind of way.

"Opening day of what?" Joel wanted to know. His plate had been cleaned to the last crumb. "Can I have some more pie?"

"You may," Lovina told him. "Maybe Rebecca would cut you a small piece." He followed the girl out to the kitchen, while Lovina repeated, "Opening day of what?"

"Hunting season," Daniel told her. "The whole county is likely already crawling with hunters, and four-wheel-drive trucks, and giant RVs, and all manner of *Englisch* who have flown in for guided hunts at the dude ranch. It won't be safe for a cow to raise its head until the end of November."

Lovina felt her cheeks go cold as the color faded from her face. "Will Joel be safe here?"

The boy returned with his plate and wiggled into the chair next to Rebecca. "'Course I'll be safe, Mamm. Cows don't look a bit like deer, and neither do I."

"Is that what they're hunting?" Oh goodness, could this get any worse?

"Deer and elk," Reuben said. His brows furrowed in concern. "Are you all right, child?"

"I—I—" She felt as though she was going to faint.

Daniel got up and went into the kitchen. He filled a glass of water and handed it to her. "Drink this."

The cold water was delicious, and when she'd downed it all and handed him the glass, she felt a little better. "I'm sorry. I feel foolish. But—"

"My *dat* was killed by a hunter," Joel said with his mouth full, and the Miller family fell utterly silent, staring at him in dismay.

Chapter 16

IT FELT AS THOUGH ALL the air had suddenly been sucked from the room. Naomi covered her lips with her fingers, and Malena's mouth dropped open.

"A hunter?" Reuben repeated. "How did such a thing happen?"

"Dat, it could be that Lovina doesn't want to talk about it," Daniel said. He was frowning, but not in disapproval. In concern.

"Neh, it's fine. It was just a shock—I didn't know—" Lovina took a deep breath to stop herself from babbling. "As Joel said, Mose was hunting. In Lebanon County, with his brothers. They go every year. They were in a thickly forested area, and not—I mean, they didn't have the blaze orange vests on, and—"

"And an *Englisch* man on the other side of the ravine saw the bushes moving and thought he was a deer," Joel finished.

"Ach, neh," Naomi breathed. "How awful for you both."

"It was," Lovina got out. She had nightmares about it yet. So did Joel. But for vastly different reasons.

Unlike her son, it had taken months before the rage she had felt toward her husband for going when she had begged him not to had subsided even a little. She had chosen a good man, a gentle man, a *safe* man, only to discover he had a stubborn streak a mile deep when it came to his brothers. Their annual hunting trip was only one of many sacrifices she had learned must be made if she was to submit to her husband.

"What happened to the other man?" Reuben asked. "The hunter?"

"I felt very sorry for him," Lovina admitted. "He came to the shop, weeping. It was terrible. But as the sheriff said, he was not an experienced hunter, and our men were not properly dressed. There was fault on both sides. When the sheriff asked me if I wanted to press charges, I said no. It was *Gott*'s will. And Mose would not want two families ruined because of a mistake, even such a dreadful one."

A silence fell. Then Daniel said, "I'll go to Libby alone, and find out what you want to know, Lovina."

But she shook her head. "I'd be grateful for the company, but it's my responsibility. I can pay for tickets on the spot."

And so, after a restless night, at midmorning the next day she found herself sitting on Daniel's left as he guided one of their buggy horses, a mare named Hester, down the lane.

"The buggy horses aren't named after flowers?" she said, trying for normal conversation.

"*Neh.* Cattle horses are one thing, because they don't leave the ranch except to go to the allotments. Buggy horses are another. Dat didn't see himself saying, 'Whoa, Anemone' when he came to a stop sign in town."

She couldn't help but smile at the thought of weathered, muscular Reuben Miller doing such a thing.

"It's *gut* to see you smile, Lovina," Daniel said gruffly. "After last evening, I thought you'd ask me to take you straight to the train station."

"Well, you are," she pointed out.

"*Ja,* but I thought you might want me to put you both on the train, too."

"Learning it was opening day was just such a shock," she admitted. "I suppose I should have expected it—it is October, and Montana is a big draw for hunters. I feel like an idiot for making such a scene."

"You lost your husband in a terrible, shocking way. No one thinks you made a scene."

They were coming to the end of the field where Joel had spotted Susan skiing. Now the vista opened up and she could see two pickup trucks parked outside a cattle gate on the opposite side of the road. A chill arrowed through her stomach.

"You meant it, didn't you, Daniel? That Joel would be safe with all these hunters around?"

He had seen the trucks, too. "They'll come up to the house and ask if they can hunt on our land, but Dat never gives permission. He won't have the cattle disturbed before the trucks come."

"And after the calves are gone?" As they passed the gate, she saw the pickups were deserted. The rancher on that side must have given them permission—they and their rifles were probably miles away, up in the foothills.

"Well, you'll be gone by then, won't you?"

"*Ja,*" she said slowly. "I suppose I will."

Daniel clucked to Hester, who picked up her pace on the level road. "Even if Dat normally gave permission, he wouldn't now. Not when a grieving widow is involved, losing her husband in such a way. That would be cruel."

"I'm not grieving anymore," came out of her mouth before the thought had barely formed in her mind.

He glanced at her in surprise before his attention turned back to the road. Two miles along and the traffic was noticeably heavier now.

"I mean—I mean—oh, I don't know what I mean," Lovina said, shaking her head in its black away bonnet. But this was Daniel. Surely she could be honest with him, if no one else? "The truth of the matter is, I was so angry with Mose that there was barely any room left for grief."

"He can't be blamed for a rookie hunter's mistake, surely."

"It's not a matter of blame. Of course I don't blame him." How to say this without his thinking less of her? "But I asked him not to go on that trip. Asked, begged, demanded. None of it did any good. He went against my wishes, and that is what makes me angry. He did not think of me, or of Joel and how much he needs his father. He thought only of himself and this stupid trip he and his brothers just had to take every year."

"He had gone every other year?"

"*Ja,* like clockwork."

"So what made last year different?"

Here it came. "I don't think you want to hear it, Daniel."

"I don't if you don't want to tell me. But we used to be a shoulder for the other to lean on. I hope that might still be true, if nothing else."

It was the first time he had willingly referred to that summer. And he spoke the truth. Now was her chance to do the same.

She took a deep breath, as though she were about to jump into a lake far below. "Last year was different because I had just learned I was expecting. I had a feeling that I could not shake—a fear that no amount of prayer could take away. And when they'd been gone only four days and I opened the door to find his oldest brother on the doorstep—with the news—" Her throat closed and she had to swallow to clear it. "Less than a week afterward, I miscarried. The day after the funeral."

At his sharp intake of breath, it seemed that

the wave of rage rose up inside her—a towering wave she could not control. It rose—it crashed down—she struck the polished dashboard of the buggy and shouted, "I *wanted* our baby! I cannot forgive him for taking her from me, too! That could not have been *Gott's* will!"

She burst into tears of anger and shame, sobbing into her hands. Wordlessly, Daniel guided Hester on to the grassy shoulder of the road and set the brake. Then he took her into his arms, holding her while she cried—deep, grinding sobs that came up out of that dark place where she had been pressing down her rage and sorrow.

They were not pressed down now. They were a cup running over—a storm unleashed—and she could not stop the tears. But oh, it felt wonderful good to be held as she cried. To realize he was untying her bonnet so that she could bury her face without hindrance in his strong, warm shoulder. To clutch the wool lapels of his coat in both her hands as though to let go would mean she drowned. To know that the big, capable hands slowly stroking her back would not let her go until she was ready.

To simply let go, knowing that he had already caught her before she fell.

DANIEL SENSED the moment when the force of the gale within Lovina reached its peak and began to ebb. He had never been so grateful for the good Lord's guidance, being in exactly the right place at the right time and able to give her what she needed. Not a solution, not bracing words, not judgement for the dreadful thing that she had finally managed to expel ... but simply to hold her.

To love her.

Oh, he knew it now. He had never stopped loving her, sinner that he was, not for the whole time she'd been married. He'd been trying for nine years not to love her, and sometimes he even thought he'd succeeded. Then a snippet of news would come in a letter, or a woman would look at him with a hopeful gaze, and he would feel it again. That wave of grief and loneliness and a strange, immovable loyalty that had kept him so long from courting any other woman.

But the last thing she needed was the burden of his love when she still had so much to work through. She had to leave the Circle M, as he had had to leave Whinburg Township years ago, for perfectly good reasons. And while he might wonder at the will of *der Herr* in bringing them together again only to force them apart, it was not for him to question. His job was simply to act as his heart was directed.

And right now, his heart directed him to hold her for as long as she wanted him to.

He had no idea how much time had passed before she finally lifted her head. His arms loosened as she pulled away a little.

"I deed a tissue," she said thickly. "I'b a bess."

He handed her his hankie, thankful that for once he'd brought a clean one with him. After blowing her nose with a sound like a foghorn, she wiped her face and took a deep breath. Then she reached up to swipe a finger across his cheek. "You're crying."

He was? He brushed a palm across his face and was surprised when it came away wet. "I guess I am."

"Do you think less of me now that I've shown you what a sinner I am?"

"We are all sinners," he told her softly.

"Yes, but only a special few are so angry at their dead husbands that they can't control themselves."

"How do you feel, after the storm?"

She paused, as though to take stock of her

emotions. "After the storm," she said, "the still, small voice." Her gaze rose to his. "The heavenly Father's ... and yours. *Denki* for being here for me."

"I'm glad I was. So is Hester."

He'd hoped to hear a gurgle of laughter bubbling out of her, and he was rewarded. "Poor Hester. Goodness knows what she would have done if I'd had the reins. We might have been racing all the way to Libby."

It gladdened his heart to see her sense of humor glimmer out. He hadn't seen nearly enough of it since she'd been here, and now he had an idea why.

"In answer to your question, *neh*, I don't think less of you. Far from it. Those are terrible burdens to carry—losing your husband, Joel losing his father, losing your little *Boppli*. But God has promised peace after the storm. A rainbow after the flood."

She gazed into the distance before them, where the road curved between two pine-covered hills. Mountain Home lay just beyond, in the valley formed by Siksika Lake, the magnificent lake that Reuben often paused to take in during roundup.

"It's strange," she said in a wondering tone. "I

should be disgusted with myself for saying those words out loud to you. But mostly I feel ... lighter. As though letting them out somehow lanced a nasty boil inside of me."

That sense of lightness he'd felt before returned tenfold. "That is *gut* news. And now?"

"Now I think it's a *gut* thing that it's the season of asking forgiveness. I think I have more to be sorry for than Joel does with poor Elijah Peachy."

"But who will you send your letter to?" He was only half teasing.

"Mose," she said, surprising him again. "I think I will write the letter to him. Express every last drop from that boil, no matter how many pages it takes. And then take them all downstairs and put them in the stove."

"And after the fire?"

She gazed up at him. "The scripture says that God is not in the fire. But I hope I will hear that still, small voice, and be comforted."

"I have faith that He will," Daniel said. More than anything in the world, he wanted to take her in his arms again. To assure her that if she wanted it, he would be there for her whenever she needed him, and even when she didn't.

But it was too soon.

When he finally did embrace her, he wanted

her to come to him for herself, because their being together filled her with joy. Not now, when the last of the storm her husband had caused inside her was still muttering on the horizon, moving off but still audible and flickering with lightning. He wanted that moment to be about him and Lovina, not Lovina and Mose.

So he settled the buggy blanket over her knees and took up the reins. "I suppose we should get to Libby and do what we said we'd do, if you're to be back in time for Sisters' Day."

"I wouldn't want to explain to your family that I still don't know about the train because we never got there," she agreed. "We'd never hear the end of it."

"My mother and sisters don't need any fuel to add to that fire, sure and certain." He shook the reins over Hester's back to remind her that they weren't there to eat grass, but to get going. She snorted and the buggy lurched into motion back on to the asphalt.

They passed through the town of Mountain Home, where sure enough, the streets were alive with pickup trucks and every second person was decked out in blaze orange. Despite the fact that her hand crept into the crook of his elbow and gripped it like a vise, Lovina did her best not to show her anxiety.

"This is quite the town," she said. "It looks like the Old West."

He smiled, admiring her for trying even though her voice was strained. He kept his own easy and conversational. "It does, at that. Some of these are the original buildings, more than a hundred years old, and some are just here to make the tourists and the hunters' wives happy." He pointed out the quilt store, the bakery, the smithy, and the market, all owned and operated by Amish folks in Little Joe's flock.

"I feel badly now that Malena couldn't come to run her errand at the quilt shop," she said, sounding more relaxed as they passed homes and the public school, an area where there were fewer pickups with out-of-state license plates. "There were beautiful quilts in the window of the shop— and two *Englisch* women going in to see them as we passed."

"Don't feel too badly," he told her as they left the town behind and took the road down to Libby. "God wanted you to lance that boil, and you couldn't have done it with her in the buggy."

"No, I'm glad that if anyone had to witness it,

it was you. *Denki*, Daniel, for being such a *gut* friend."

He smiled back, content to let that be enough for now. The five miles between Mountain Home and Libby seemed to go by in a moment as he put their conversation back on a less serious footing, pointing out the Amish properties and telling her about the families who lived there. The town of Libby was larger, its roads busier, and since the church here was on the fancy side, they no longer used buggies. But at the train station, which all the local Amish used, there was still a fence rail for the buggy horses. When he brought Hester to a stop in the parking lot, Lovina slid the door open and hopped down before he could set the brake and come around to help her. But it was only to loop the leading rein over the rail. And as they walked into the station with its half-timbered walls, it was all he could do to keep a little distance between them and not take her hand.

A *gut* friend was a *gut* start. But he wanted more. Much more. He was only now beginning to understand how difficult it was going to be, to give her space and time.

The eastbound train, it turned out, left at 5:21 a.m. each morning and arrived in Chicago the next day. The fare was nearly two hundred dollars for one person, and that wasn't even for a sleeper. Lovina thanked the ticket agent and turned back to Daniel, troubled.

"I didn't realize it would be so much," she said. "It will take more money than I have left, and doesn't even get me to Lancaster, only Chicago."

"Shall we go back to Mountain Home and check the bus routes at the library?"

But that yielded even less satisfaction. The routes were so confusing and numerous that it might take two weeks to get home that way, with a motel to pay for in between buses.

"I need to think on this," Lovina said at last, leaving the library's free terminal to the next patron. "It means another trip to town, I suppose, and I'm sorry for that."

"Don't be," he said easily, trying to hide his delight that she wouldn't be leaving in the morning. "We're up and down the highway all the time. It's not so far."

And now he had her to himself again for the two miles back to the ranch.

"We might think of alternatives for Joel until you can see your way clear," he said, once they had passed through Mountain Home and were once again on the familiar county road. Soon their own acres would come into view, a sight that always filled him with quiet happiness. "Can he go to school here for as long as he needs to?"

She turned a little on the bench to stare at him in surprise. "Is that possible?"

"I don't know why not. It would only be temporary. Surely they could find him a seat, and he already knows one or two of the *Kinner*."

"How far away is the schoolhouse?"

"If you turn left instead of right out of our lane, it's about a mile up the road, at the junction where the turn takes people to the dude ranch. Little Joe donated the property several years ago, so the school is fairly new. With the money from the auction that year, we hired the Meadowlark folks to build a nice log schoolhouse with a long porch, insulated and designed to be snug in winter."

"They built your family's place, too, didn't they?"

He nodded. "Mine, too. They do *gut* work. And they understand how Amish homes are supposed to be."

"I'll talk to Anna and Katherine this afternoon. Anna's eldest is old enough to go to school, so she would know. And it would only be for a short time."

Daniel knew she had to return to her home,

her business. Joel had to return to his own school and his family and friends. But that knowledge didn't douse the warm glow inside him at the certainty that, for at least a few days, she would stay.

He just needed to find a way to convince her to stay for good and ever.

Chapter 17

LOVINA WASN'T ABOUT to mention the possibility of school to Joel, but she needn't have worried. He was still out in the fields with the Miller men, checking calves. Perhaps an essay on the calves would be his assignment for tonight, to include as many difficult spelling words as she could think of. But for now, as she rattled back down the lane on the way to Bishop Joe's ranch and Sisters' Day, her thoughts whirled with train fares, bus routes, and what had happened between herself and Daniel.

As Hester made the left turn onto the road, her mind calmed as she reached for that source of help that never failed.

Dear Lord, I thank You for sending Daniel to be

with me as You dealt once and for all with my heart. I know I've prayed many times for Your help in removing that ugly darkness, and though I may have turned Daniel away from me forever with my wickedness, I pray that I have not. Help me now to walk a different path, one blessed by Your light instead of my own grief and despair. Help me to remember the good, and put away the evil. Mose was only human, made by Your hand, and he gave me many good years—and Joel. Help me to look forward, not back, from within the center of Your will. Bless little Karina, I pray, and tell her I love her always. In Jesus' holy name, amen.

She pulled up in her cousin the bishop's yard, where one of his sons came out to greet her warmly and put Hester up for the afternoon. She collected the pan of frosted apple cake that Rebecca had thoughtfully baked for the occasion while she had been out that morning, and went into the house.

Sadie, her daughter Ruby, and her daughters-in-law Anna and Katherine welcomed Lovina in a flurry of greetings and kisses, and she was soon introduced to Cousin Joe's sister Rosemary Wengerd Eicher, who had arrived from St. Ignatius only the day before for a week's visit.

"It's like a little family reunion," Cousin Rosemary said happily, settling at the quilting frame.

"I never thought I would get to see you, Lovina. How are Elmer and Grace?"

"They're very well, as far as I know," Lovina said, hoping that she wouldn't ask after them further. She saw her foster parents about once a year, and their correspondence was more dutiful than regular. "I haven't been home in several weeks—up until recently, we'd been touring the national parks with the Troyers from Willow Creek."

"The *Englisch* van broke down and by *Gott's* hand Lovina and her boy Joel wound up here," Sadie explained. "It's a lucky thing, too, for the Troyers were called home unexpectedly. And here we are."

"But she's not staying with us?" Rosemary looked puzzled as she measured out an arm's length of thread, snipped it, and threaded her needle.

"*Neh*, she was invited to stay for roundup at the Circle M," Sadie said comfortably. "It's quite an education for her boy, and more *Youngie* there than here, now."

"But surely there is more room here now that the boys are grown." Rosemary didn't seem inclined to leave the subject alone. "And Ruby here is a single woman. Still."

Ruby ducked her head and began to rock her stitches onto her needle as though her life depended on it.

"*Ja*, that is true, but it has all worked out." With this pronouncement, Sadie loaded nine stitches onto her own needle. "How do you like this pattern, Rosemary? It's called Flying Home. Ever seen it made up before?"

"*Neh*, I haven't." Rosemary loaded her own needle. "You've done a nice job."

Nice wasn't the word for it. "It's lovely," Lovina said, busy on a spray of leaves that formed a wreath in the center of a block. "I love how the flying geese extend out into the borders in their V formations."

"That was Malena Miller's idea," Ruby confided. "It wasn't in the pattern, and I wasn't sure it would work. But Malena could see it so clearly in her mind that when she sketched it out, I could see right away how pretty it would be."

"She's a wonderful *gut* quilter," Anna agreed. "As are you, Ruby."

"And this is to be a wedding quilt, you say?" Rosemary asked. "Do I know whose? It can't be anyone in the Wengerd family or I'd have heard. Unless ... Ruby, is there something you're keeping from me?"

"*Neh, Aendi,*" Ruby said softly. A slow color burned into her cheeks, while the rhythm of her stitches never faltered.

"Someone in the neighborhood?"

All four of the Wengerd women kept their eyes on their work, their needles moving steadily through the layers of fabric and backing. "They haven't told me whether they have someone in mind," Lovina ventured, when no one answered. "But surely the bishop will make at least one new announcement in church before long."

"Wedding season will be here before we know it, and Christmas around the corner," Rosemary agreed. "But surely you have an idea of who might be making a visit to the bishop, Sadie? You haven't so many *Youngie* here that a courting couple might escape your notice."

"*Neh,*" Sadie said. "But if a couple *were* to speak to the bishop it would not be my place to say, even to my nearest and dearest."

"You do have an idea!" Rosemary pounced on this as the next best thing to a confession. "You may be the bishop's wife, but I am the bishop's sister. I won't tell a soul."

Katherine and Anna looked ready to burst, while Ruby rocked her needle in and out, in and out. Anna's cheeks had gone scarlet with the effort to hold in either laughter or the answer that Rosemary was angling for.

Lovina smiled down at her handiwork. So there *was* a bride with this quilt in her future. Lucky girl. Imagine having something as lovely as this gracing your bed. And its theme of flying geese coming home would fit in so well in a home built of logs, like the Miller place. Into her mind flashed an image of a large, snug bedroom in a beautiful home looking out into these mountains, with the summer sun shining in on this quilt and a baby learning to roll over in the middle of the bed. She and Daniel laughing on either side of the child while Joel sat cross-legged on the end, enjoying the antics of his little *bruder* or *schweschder*.

"Lovina?"

The vision vanished. She fumbled her needle and dropped it. Looking up, she realized that all the women were staring at her.

"Sorry?" she said. "I lost my needle. Just a moment." She fished it up at the end of its thread and ran it through to the top side. "Did I miss something?"

"You were a hundred miles away," Rosemary told her. "I *said*, what are your plans now, after your dear husband's passing? Are you going back to Whinburg, to be closer to Grace and Elmer?"

Never on earth. Lovina bit back the response and shook her head instead. "I still have the antique shop, and I like Willow Creek. We plan to stay there."

"You'd do better to ask *der Himmlischer Vater* what his plans are," Sadie said, the twinkle in her eyes showing Lovina that she didn't intend a lecture, but motherly advice. "What if He has brought you out west for His purposes?"

"That *Englisch* taxi-van broke down where it did for a reason," Ruby pointed out, her needle now flashing at a speed Lovina could only envy.

Lovina had to laugh. *"Ja,* so we could spend the night on the ground on the side of a mountain, and be stuck in a freak blizzard, and eat more cherry pie than is *gut* for us. But I haven't figured out what my lessons are in that yet. Other than I need Naomi Miller's recipe."

"There is still a reason," Ruby said earnestly, looking up. "You must wait on God to find it out."

It was time to change the subject. "I meant to ask you, Anna, about the school here. If it takes longer than I believe it will to arrange travel back to Whinburg Township, do you think the teacher would object to Joel's joining the scholars here for a short time?"

Anna's eyebrows rose, and she flashed a

glance at her mother-in-law. "I don't see why not. I was there at the beginning of the school year for parents' night, and it seemed they had one or two empty desks. Your Joel is in third grade?"

"*Ja.* It wouldn't be for long. I'm just worried he'll fall behind, is all. My little worksheets in the evenings are no substitute for a day of lessons on all subjects."

Anna reached over to touch the back of her hand. "You can leave it with me. I'll speak to our teacher, Hannah Fischer, tomorrow when I walk over with my Thomas. He's just gone into first grade. I'm sure it will be all right. When he starts, Joel can walk with us."

Lovina felt a gush of relief. "Oh, *denki*. I might have arrangements made by then, but if I don't, at least I will know that Joel is looked after. Though he might not agree with me that it's a wonderful *gut* idea."

The ladies laughed, and the talk turned to family news, and the doings of the community. Lovina was so entertained and found such comfort in her relatives' company that she succeeded in putting aside the warmth and joy of that brief vision she'd had of the wedding quilt.

A vision of a life that could not be hers. So she had best chase such thoughts out of her head, and turn her mind to solving the problem of getting herself and Joel back home.

Their real home.

———

DEAR MOSE,

Do you remember the day you proposed to me? I was not quite twenty, and had joined church that spring. You said that if I married you, you would care for and provide for me so that I would never have to feel afraid and unloved again. That you would keep me and our future children safe. That you would never leave me until God saw fit to take you home.

I suppose you kept that last promise, at least.

But I have had a terrible time with the ones you didn't keep. The ones you broke by putting yourself in harm's way. While I cannot and will not blame God for allowing it, I have blamed you for not thinking of me. Is that reasonable? I no longer know. All I know is that you had a responsibility to us. Joel and me. And to Karina, the tiny life we created together who never even got the chance to breathe.

Yes, I called her Karina in my heart, and I never got the chance to tell you that, either.

So you see, Mose, in reality you broke all your promises. I have felt afraid and unloved ever since you went with your brothers instead of staying for my sake. I have not felt safe for one minute, not until lately. And you left me, though I know you never wanted to.

But now, things have changed. Something happened to me yesterday that let me release all these bad thoughts to God, who will throw them into the sea of forgetfulness and never cast them up to me. And do you know why? I told you about Daniel, didn't I? But I didn't tell you everything. Those things are between him and me. But I did say that when he proposed marriage, the summer before I married you, he wanted to take me back with him to Montana. I was filled with a terrible, irrational fear because I didn't know what our life would be like. I was afraid. I had no faith—in God, or in Daniel. I was like you, Mose, and I didn't listen to my heart.

The result was only disaster.

But unlike you, dear man, I have been given a second chance. I have seen what Daniel's life is like in some small measure, and I'm no longer that frightened Maedel you married. I have discovered that I am capable of looking after myself instead of clinging to someone who can do it for me. I might even be the kind of woman who could live a life out here. Maybe. I'm not sure how I can find that out for sure and certain, but if it is His will, God will show me.

3

I suppose all this is to say that I am finally able to forgive you, husband. I hope that you will forgive me for being that clingy, frightened woman, barely more than a child, who demanded everything you had to give and more while giving so little herself. At least we gave each other Joel. He is the treasure that lights my days. I will always be grateful to you for being such a good father. He loves you as a boy should, without fear and without judgment.

Good-bye, Mose. I will look back on our days together with fondness and gratitude. And I will look forward with love and faith. That, too, is God's gift to us.

Dei Fraa,
Lovina

Chapter 18

IT WAS WELL after nine o'clock on Wednesday evening when Daniel heard the soft pad of stocking feet going downstairs. A moment later, the kitchen door to the basement closed.

Lovina.

After their worksheet that evening, which had been about checking calves and contained far more difficult words than the events of the day deserved, she had set Joel to the task of writing his letter to Elijah Peachey. One thing he could say about her was that she didn't waste time. There was no putting off her own letter to her late husband, either. While she hadn't let Joel see it, of course, she had sat at the kitchen table across from him and been a good example to her son. Though it had taken an hour, and she had filled three sheets to his one, the task had been finished at last. After addressing the envelopes to teacher and to friend, Joel had gone off to help the twins with the jigsaw puzzle.

Daniel had watched from behind the pages of *The Western News*, the Lincoln County paper, as she had signed her letter, folded it in three, and slipped it into her apron pocket.

Now he pushed the quilt aside and rose without waking his brother. He pulled on his pants and the top of his winter long johns, and tiptoed down the stairs himself.

He found her watching the bright flames consume the paper. The scent of smoke from her opening the door was already fading. When charred ashes fell among the logs banked for the night, she remained standing, holding out her hands to the warmth like his mother did, though the basement was cozy.

"Here," he said quietly. He pulled up the garden bench that Alden Stolzfus had made a couple of winters ago, its seat and back made of slats of California redwood, its arms and legs wrought iron that formed the Circle M brand. "This usually sits on the front porch in summer, along with Mamm's rocking chair and an ancient wicker monstrosity that Dat can't seem to part with."

"*Denki*," she said, and sat. She didn't seem surprised to see him, and her acceptance was an encouragement.

He had the choice to pull up the squeaky, creaky wicker chair or seat himself beside her. There was no choice, really. Not after they'd spent a morning in the buggy in far closer quarters than these.

"It's done?" he asked, though he knew the answer.

"*Ja*, it's done. And I feel the way I do when I come to the end of a book. I close it, and I feel satisfied, as though there is nothing else I want to read."

"Or write, in this case."

She nodded. "Nothing left to say. I poured it all out, and now it's gone. As it should be."

"I'm glad."

"I will be glad, I suppose. For now, I'm ... at peace. And that is rare enough in my life that I've just been standing here, marveling at it."

He straightened. Maybe he'd made a mistake in joining her. "Would you rather I went back to bed and left you alone?"

"Poor man, you were there for the noisy part."

She gave him a sideways smile. "It would be too bad to send you away when I got to the quiet part."

He chuckled. "I'm happy to be here for both. We appreciate peace around here."

"I can imagine. But as long as you have it in your heart and your home, you can carry it with you anywhere, can't you?"

How wise she was. "Even in the high country, when I've lost a calf to a wolf, or the ice in the pond refuses to thaw until May, or the city folks wander onto our land from the dude ranch and forget to close the gates, I can still have peace."

"All those things have happened?"

"All in one year. And more besides."

She shook her head, half amused, half horrified. "Yet you love it."

"I do. Well, except for the dude ranch. I wouldn't mind a bit if they packed up and went back to Los Angeles or wherever it is they're from. They're nice folks, but they have their hands full sometimes with the people who come for 'the true western experience.'" With his hands dangling between his knees, he made quote marks with his fingers.

"No danger of the Circle M opening to tourists for 'the true Amish experience'?" She made her own quote marks, and he found himself wishing he could take the hand she lowered to her lap. Entwine his fingers through hers, palm to palm.

"Don't say that." He pretended to shudder. "Though I've heard that out in Colorado, one of the *Englisch* dude ranches hires our *Youngie* for just that kind of experience."

"I know," she said, surprising him. "The *Dokterfraa*'s son from Willow Creek and one or two of the others were out there someplace, near Westcliffe. The boys worked with the horses on guided pack trips, and the girls were *Mauds* and cooks. I heard that the *Englisch* owners were taking pictures of them and using them in their advertising. But the husband put a stop to that eventually, once he found out what his wife was doing."

"Best for our folk not to go back there," he said. "If they want to work, they can come here, like I told Joel."

With a smile, she said, *"Ja,* he said you had. Luckily, it will be eight years before I have to have that conversation."

"I was serious," he said quietly. "He'd be welcome no matter how old he is. And you, too."

"Next time I'll be helping in the kitchen at

roundup, not on horseback," she said lightly.

"I didn't mean just as a cowhand." His heart began to pound, and he wondered if she could see it. "You're welcome to visit us anytime, just for yourself."

"That's very kind of you, Daniel," she said, ducking her chin in that endearing way she had. "But you might take it back when you find out my preparations for Communion aren't quite finished yet."

"You mean you have another letter to write?" Who to? A man? It had never occurred to him until this moment that there might be someone waiting in the wings back home. Waiting for her mourning to end and, as the saying went, for her to look about and take notice.

Now, instead of galloping, his heart might just stop altogether.

"I can write it if you like," she said slowly. "Or I can just ask your forgiveness now."

The breath went out of him in a rush. "Oh." His head reeled just a little with relief.

"I know you don't like to talk about the past. But Daniel, I feel that if I don't, I won't be able to go forward. God needs us to step out on his promises, and I don't think I can do that unless you forgive me."

No, he didn't like to talk about the past. It hurt too much to exhume some things. And yet, she had proven that it was healthy to exhume others, no matter how ugly.

"Forgive you for what?" he managed.

She slid a glance his way, the dim firelight glancing off her cheekbone, her nose, turning the strands of hair escaping from under her *Kapp* the deep gold of ripe wheat. "For what I said that night you proposed."

He could say a lot of things. *I've forgotten. It doesn't matter. There's nothing to forgive.*

But he hadn't, and it still did, and there was. Or at least, there had been until recently.

Until yesterday.

But he couldn't say that, either. The time wasn't ripe.

———

IF HE DIDN'T SAY something, Lovina thought she might come right out of her skin. This had to be the most difficult conversation she'd ever attempted. What would she do if he simply got up and left, and her sitting here with all the words bottled up inside?

She'd better get them out in the open before that happened.

"Maybe you—" Her throat closed, and she tried again. "Maybe you remember the other day, when I told you a little about my childhood?"

"About your friends the barn cats?"

She nodded. "That was the best of it. That, and school. Onkel Elmer's was probably the fifth or sixth home I had lived in during the years after my parents died. Mostly it was family who took me in, but for one reason or another, couldn't keep me for good and ever. In one of them I read that book, *Anne of Green Gables*. I actually found myself looking in the glass of the china cabinet in the *Eck* for my own Katie Maurice." She glanced at him. "That was Anne's imaginary friend in the same situation."

He nodded. "The twins had that book from the library once."

"I came to Onkel Elmer's thinking the farm was my own Green Gables, but the only similarity was that the house was painted white." She huffed a laugh. "No green gables there—the bishop insisted that all house trim be painted black. Not to disparage them. They did their best when they already had a big family. But it was difficult. I was a fearful little child, and it only got worse."

"Fearful of what?" His voice was quiet, almost gruff. "Did they hurt you?"

She sighed. "Not in body. But in spirit there were a thousand little wounds. I was afraid of nearly everything, I guess. Of leaving. Saying hallo, because that only meant saying good-bye eventually. Of feeling too comfortable in a bed, because I would soon have to get used to another one. Of loving the flowers in the garden, because I wouldn't be there to pick them by the time they bloomed. Oh, so many things."

"It's a wonder you survived."

"Oh, I was taken care of. Fed, clothed, taken to church, sent to school. I wanted for none of the basics of life. Only the things that make it rich and happy and satisfying." She tilted her head toward him, watching the glow of the fire. "Until I met you."

After a moment, he said, "How did you come to be in Whinburg Township and not Smicksburg?"

"I went to visit a cousin, my suitcase packed full of everything I owned, which wasn't much. I never went back. I got a job instead. My cousin and her husband were happy to rent me a room—

a basement room that was dark and poky, but it was all mine, and had a bathroom to boot. And then you came for the summer, and it seemed that for once in my life, I could be like other girls. More. Because no one had ever loved a boy the way I loved you. For a few short months, I forgot to be afraid."

Slowly, he ran his hands over his face, for all the world like wiping away the pictures on a slate. "I wish I'd known."

"And that's part of why I must ask your forgiveness. For keeping all that from you—being ashamed of it."

"You had nothing to be ashamed of." He sat up. "Don't ever think that."

"I don't, now. In fact, I've come to feel sorry for that succession of relatives who had no idea what to do with a silent, sensitive child. How to make her feel comfortable. Wanted. They did their best, but when I think of Joel being left in such a situation, I—" Her throat closed again.

"Don't think of it," Daniel said roughly. "He is safe, and loved, and you have done that for him. And while you don't need to ask my forgiveness, you have it anyway. Now that I know, I see that poor little *Maedel* you were, being asked to go somewhere she's hardly even heard of to be something she doesn't know how to be. A ranch wife. A mother. A daughter- and sister-in-law."

"All I knew of Montana was that it had avalanches and bears. I couldn't even imagine your parents or brothers and sisters." She lifted a hand to encompass the house. "Couldn't imagine this. How *wonderbaar* it all is. Do you have any idea how many blessings *Gott* has showered on you?"

"If I didn't before, I surely do now," he said, looking into her face and meaning every word.

"I never felt safe," she said in a wondering tone. "Never once, and it was worse after I sent you away. Much worse than flowers or barn cats or school friends. I felt I would never know love again. And then came Mose."

He waited, and she appreciated that.

"I had known him since I'd arrived. His family lived on the farm next to where my cousins were, and I saw him in church. After you left, he asked if he could court me." She must confess it all, now that she had begun. "I had wounded myself worse than any of my relatives ever could by sending you away. I didn't really know him. All I could see was that he was safe. He'd never been out of Pennsylvania, not even for a holiday. The family had been on that farm for generations, and while he didn't farm, he'd already established the antique business. We didn't enjoy many of the same things, but at the time, that didn't matter. He wasn't you. And he would never leave me or make me pull up my roots and go where I didn't want to go. And so..."

"You married him."

She nodded. "You left in September. We married in February. He never even knew you and I had courted until I told him during our honeymoon visits."

"And by then it didn't matter."

"It still mattered to me." She sighed. "I was a terrible wife. Not because I couldn't cook or keep house—any girl brought up by Aendi Grace could do both things well. But because I married him while I still loved you. That was a sin. And I went ahead and committed it anyway—because once again, I was afraid."

A silence fell, broken by the *pop* of the wood in the stove as the flames found a pocket of pitch.

"Did you make him happy?" he asked, surprising her again.

"As happy as good cooking, a smile, and a willingness to work could make a man, I suppose," she said slowly. "And I did find happiness in the peace of that life. Confidence, too. Then, when Joel was born, he transformed my world and it has never been the same since. I never knew such an all-consuming love could exist, even after you." She looked up quickly. "I mean—"

And he laughed. "It's all right. I know what you meant."

"Do you think less of me?" She could hardly get the question out, but she needed to know. "For marrying someone else so quickly, and for such unworthy reasons?"

"I did for a long time after I heard," he said slowly, as though considering every word for its truth. "I knew Mose a little, and just couldn't believe that the beautiful, golden girl I had fallen in love with could possibly be happy with someone like him. It was like a daffodil trying to be happy with a mossy stone."

He could not have described the two of them any more perfectly, Lovina thought. And yet, the stone could not be moved, and protected the daffodil from the wind. There was something to be said for that.

"But now," he went on, "I see that he was what you needed then. Not me, and the life I offered." He glanced at her. "There *are* bears and avalanches, by the way."

"I never doubted that." It felt so good to be

able to smile. A real one, not just a curve of the lips that could hide the truth.

"And maybe I understand now in a way I could not have then. I grew up in a home so completely different from all the homes you lived in. For me, even with the bears and avalanches, there is not so much danger that my family can't face it together. We face everything together. We back each other up. The little boys at school knew better than to pick on Joshua. Zach and Adam would land on them like hawks on a mouse and they'd run for the hills. And when the twins got into trouble—which was a lot—it was me they came to for help."

"I hope that someday Joel can have a family like that," she said dreamily. A second later, she was horrified at herself. "Daniel, I hope— I mean, that sounded presumptuous and very forward. I hope you don't think I meant anything by it."

She could feel his withdrawal like the tide going out.

"*Neh*, not at all." He got up. "Good night, Lovina."

"Good night," she said faintly, and wondered how, in her half an hour of apologies, she could have managed to hurt him again when all she wanted to do was to tell him she loved him.

Chapter 19

THEY HAD COME SO CLOSE.

If Daniel had opened his mouth and told her he still loved her, it still wouldn't be welcome. She had spoken in terms of friendship last night. Asked for his forgiveness, but never asked how he felt. And when she'd spoken of Joel and all she wished for him, it had been on the tip of Daniel's tongue to tell her that he could provide all that she wanted for her boy and more, if only she would say yes when he asked the question again.

I hope you don't think I meant anything by it.

He had, for about two seconds. He'd felt a great surge of happiness ... and then she'd said that and he'd realized his mistake.

The calves were halfway to being weaned, and

with Adam and Zach watching them carefully, there was no reason he couldn't spend a little time working on his house. Maybe some part of him thought he might be running away, hiding in his burrow like an injured animal. But the greater part of him just wanted to have a little space for a while. Do something constructive for his own future.

He shrugged on his coat and fitted his oldest black hat on his head, then took off at a fast walk down the cut line behind the big house. His place was about a mile away, carefully situated so that from the east windows he could see the lights of his parents' home in the distance, and they would be able to look back and see his. The house itself was all on one level, though, not like the two spacious stories and loft he had grown up in. But instead of the large attached garage that had created the L-shape in the original floor plan meant for an *Englisch* buyer, he had converted it to a wing that would accommodate four bedrooms. If he ever found the woman that God wanted for him and started a family of his own, there would be plenty of room for them. And the great room would accommodate the *Gmee* when it came their turn to host church.

It didn't take long to walk the distance, the

last hundred yards or so having been widened by the delivery trucks and construction crew as they dropped off lumber and equipment. This would be a driveway by next year. He had chosen to insulate the house's interior walls and add a layer of Sheetrock and plaster for extra warmth, leaving the big log beams of the structure exposed in all their beauty. The windows were in and insulated, but not trimmed inside yet, so he inspected them all just to make sure the snow hadn't got in where it wasn't supposed to.

He was in the back bedroom enjoying the view over the meadows when he heard an almighty crash and a cry. Had he left the door open? Were there raccoons in the house? He swung out of the as-yet-doorless door frame and pounded down the hallway to find a small boy standing in the kitchen, both hands over his mouth.

"I'm sorry, Daniel," Joel confessed. "I knocked over the bucket by accident."

It had been standing on the worktable that would become a kitchen island and sink, probably a little too close to the edge.

"It's all right," he said. "Just pick everything up and put it all back in. You can leave the bucket on the floor when you're done."

"That's a lot of nails." Joel gazed down at the mess. The nails had rolled all the way out into the living room.

"It won't take long to pick them up. Use the magnet. I'll be down there in one of the bedrooms. Come find me when you're done."

He didn't allow himself to smile until he was safely around the corner. With the magnet, the job wouldn't take long. It didn't hurt to learn about the properties of magnets, either, or about responsibility for your actions on a construction site.

When Joel joined him, he assured Daniel he'd got every last one. "With the magnet, it was kind of fun. I've never seen one like that, with a handle."

"Glad to hear it," Daniel said. "How did you know I was here?"

"I saw you go out from upstairs, and when you didn't go to the barn, I thought you might be going to your house. I wanted to see it. Is this your room?"

"*Ja*, I was selfish and took the big one with the best view. The others are for *Kinner*, when God sends them to me. Does your *mamm* know you're here?"

"I told her I was coming. She was carpet sweeping."

Satisfied that Lovina wouldn't worry, Daniel put the boy to work. "See these lengths of Sheetrock? They're all screwed in, but now they have to be taped so you can't see the seams between them under the plaster. After that, we'll put finishers on the top edges, for the same reason."

They got to work. While in the beginning Joel managed to get more tape on himself than the walls, he got the hang of it eventually. It was clear he'd never helped in this way before.

"Your *dat*, he had an antique shop, ain't so?" Daniel said. "Did you help him?"

"Sometimes." Joel released the bottom lip caught between his teeth as he carefully smoothed the tape into place with both hands. "I liked looking in barns for lanterns and old harrows and things."

"People buy old harrows? What for?" Daniel smoothed the top half, up to where the Sheetrock met the neat pine planking of the ceiling.

"To put in their gardens? I dunno. But it was fun to look. Once I found a whole clutch of baby rabbits in a hay bale. But Dat wouldn't let me keep one."

"They probably couldn't leave their mother

yet," Daniel said. "I guess you miss your *dat*. I know I'd miss mine something awful."

"*Ja,* I do. But *Gott* said that was his time, so we have to be willing."

"Did your *mamm* tell you that?"

"*Neh,* Mammi did. She cried during the whole funeral, and then got mad at Mamm for not crying enough." He knelt on the floor to get the last bit of tape smooth, then followed Daniel to the next seam. "I don't understand women."

He must not laugh, Daniel told himself sternly. "Don't worry, you're not alone."

But he did feel for Lovina. Imagine someone blaming you for not grieving enough. Had Mose's mother suspected that she had married her son out of fear, not for love? But enough love had come in the end to make Joel feel the closeness of family. That was important, surely?

After a couple of seams they had found their rhythm. When Joel's shoulders and arms got tired, he contented himself by following Daniel with the supplies, which was actually quite a help. In a couple of hours they had the two front bedrooms taped off, and were starting on the third.

"Shall we call it a day or finish these next two rooms?" he asked his helper.

"I'm thirsty."

"So am I. Lucky for us, the plumbing works, but you have to drink out of the tap. No cupboards yet means no glasses."

The sink was in, and the cupboards framed, but cabinets and countertops weren't in yet. He lifted the little boy up to drink, and then scooped cold water into his own mouth. He was just drying both their faces with his shirttail when a voice hallooed from outside.

"Daniel? Are you in there?"

Joel wrinkled up his face. "Oh no, not that Susan."

"She's a visitor in my home, so you'll welcome her politely, *nix?*"

Abashed, the boy nodded, but instead of welcoming her, he hung back in the empty alcove where the propane refrigerator would go.

"*Guder mariye*, Daniel," Susan said cheerfully. She looked about for a mat on which to wipe her feet, but found none. It was only subfloor; a little mud wouldn't do it any harm. "I dropped by the house, and the girls said I might find you out here."

Her smile might be wide and full of friendship, but still, he couldn't help but hope that she would find a *gut* man who would appreciate it more than he. And sooner rather than later.

"And what's more, all by yourself," she went on. "That doesn't happen very often." She stepped a little closer. "Maybe I could help with something? What do you plan for the kitchen?"

"He's not by himself." Joel popped into view. "If you'd like a drink of water, all we have is the tap."

Which was not the most gracious welcome, but at least the boy had done as Daniel had asked.

"Oh." Susan's voice held both dismay and surprise. "Where did you come from?"

"I've been helping Daniel tape walls. We have two more bedrooms to do."

"Have you, now?" Susan recovered quickly and turned that bright smile on both of them. "Well, many hands make light work. Lead the way, Daniel, and I'll lend you mine."

———

LOVINA FIRST REALIZED that Joel wasn't in the house when she finished sweeping all the carpets and she, Naomi, and the twins convened in the kitchen for a second cup of coffee around ten o'clock.

"He must be out with the boys checking calves," Naomi said.

But when Lovina climbed the stairs to the loft, where she could look out the big windows, she could count the riders in the distant fields. Reuben, Adam, Zachariah. No small fourth rider, not manning the gate or out by the water tank. Not anywhere.

Frowning, she went to their room, but of course he wasn't there, either. Or working on the twins' puzzle, or reading Reuben's newspaper, which had been folded neatly and put in the box for the stove.

She pushed down the flutter of panic and joined the Miller women once more. "He has to be in the barn with Joshua."

"No harm will come to him, Lovina," Naomi said. "The weather is fine today. He's a boy. If he's not with Josh, he's probably outside somewhere, exploring."

This was a new terror. "You don't think he'd wander off into the hills following some cattle trail, do you?"

Naomi had been paging through a recipe book, and now she gazed at Lovina over her readers. "Is Joel the kind of boy who would do something like that?"

"Not without telling me. He must be with Joshua."

Of course he was, she thought, striding across the yard and buttoning her coat as she went. He had to be with one of the men, and none of them had thought to let her know they were going out together. She was foolish to be concerned.

She found Joshua in the machine shed, smelling of cigarettes and doing maintenance on a flat wagon with metal wheels similar to the one her father-in-law used to take hay bales out to the cattle in winter. He was not very communicative, either, clearly wishing he was anywhere but here now that the weather had improved.

"Sorry, haven't seen him since breakfast," he said. "He's probably out somewhere exploring, or up in the orchard."

Which did not help at all. Back out in the yard, she took deep breaths. She mustn't panic. There was a perfectly reasonable explanation.

Wait a moment. There was one more person to check with before she committed herself to the climb up to the orchard. Where was Daniel?

She hunted through the barn from loft to milking pen, but the only creatures to look up and see her were the buggy horses, and the chickens busy with dust baths in the cool sunshine. Daniel was nowhere to be found.

When she wiped her feet and came into the

kitchen, Malena turned. "Goodness, you were gone for ages. You missed Susan and coffee both."

The last thing she wanted was either one. "Susan was here? Did she ride over?"

Rebecca laughed. "Cutting horses are for work—we don't ride around on them for visits or recreation. Bishop Joe draws a very firm line. No, she had the buggy. Didn't you see it?"

"I didn't notice," Lovina confessed. "I was looking for Joel. An *Englisch* car could have been parked in the yard and I probably wouldn't have seen it. Ach, I'm so worried."

"He's got to be with Daniel, then," Naomi said firmly from where she was stirring something on the stove. "He'll have lots of company this morning. Susan headed over there to see the progress on the house."

"Maybe she'll help him," Rebecca said with a sly grin at her twin. "He hasn't decided on countertops yet, but she has. Robin's-egg-blue tile, she told me, and china with yellow flowers to make a nice contrast."

"None of your nonsense," Naomi told her. "Let your poor *Bruder* make his own choice without your help."

"But he *needs* help," Malena protested. "I've never seen anyone so hopeless. Susan is just the kind of girl for him—cheerful, a good manager, and she can talk enough to make up for his saying hardly anything at all."

"A man is allowed to keep his own counsel," her mother informed her.

"Yes, but Susan is *fun*," Rebecca said. "He needs somebody like her around to lighten him up."

Lovina thought she might scream if she didn't get out of here. "Which way is Daniel's house?"

Naomi gave her directions and she headed out again. It was supposed to be a mile, but half walking and half jogging brought her to the wide vehicle track that branched off to the left in about ten minutes, and she approached the house from the rear.

Chest heaving, she stopped to catch her breath. Such a view! The meadows rolled away in front of the house, studded with deep green pines and aspens that had lost the last of their gold-coin leaves during the blizzard. The river that bordered the Miller land must have one or two tributaries, for a creek meandered through the grass, and in the distance, she could spot the river lined with poplars and cottonwoods. And the house itself ... it had been made by the same loving hands as the Miller home, that was obvious, with one floor. The foundations for a wide, welcoming deck were already in the ground. She could see past the brash newness of it to what it might be like a decade from now, with a garden in front to catch as much sunshine as possible, and meadow grass stretching to the creek, where *kinner* could run and play and fish for brook trout for supper.

Her heart had settled down, as though the view itself calmed her. She made her way over to the house, stepped up on a stump that was doing duty as a doorstep, and found herself in the kitchen.

Log beams held up the ceiling and lent warmth to the stark white of the unfinished walls. The kitchen gave straight on to the great room, whose windows let in that view as though the house were part of it. It felt as solid as a mountain, as beautiful as a forest. And it wasn't even finished.

Voices came from around the corner, and the tension in her stomach and shoulders flowed out of her on a wave of relief. She followed the sound into a hallway whose walls were up, with doors cut into the sheathing and pine planking already laid in the ceiling.

Inside the first room on the right, she found the three of them. Joel was on his knees, smoothing tape at the bottom of a seam while Daniel continued the process up to the ceiling. Susan didn't seem to be doing anything but talking, all the while gazing at the window as though she was already measuring it for curtains.

Well, that was just fine. She and Joel would be gone soon, just as quickly as she could arrange the money for train tickets, and the field would be left wide open for her.

"Joel!" His name came out much more harshly than she intended.

Her boy looked up, and Susan stopped in mid-sentence.

"Hallo, Mamm. I'm helping Daniel tape walls."

"So I see," she said, doing her best to keep her voice from trembling. "What I do not like is that you came out without telling me. I have been looking for you for an hour."

"But I did tell you!" he protested, bouncing to his feet. "When you were sweeping the carpet. I said I was going to see Daniel's house."

She stared at him. "I did not hear you." Because the carpet sweeper was old and loud, and she'd been off in a dream world populated by babies and sunlight and wedding quilts. Her face heated, though no one could possibly have known how her thoughts kept betraying her.

"I did, Mamm. I promise!"

"He told me you knew he was with me, or I'd never have let him stay all this time," Daniel said, dusting off his hands. "He's been a *gut* help, though."

That was *not* the point.

"Joel, tell your *mamm* you're sorry to have worried her," Susan said. "She's walked all the way out here thinking you were lost."

Joel got that mulish look that Lovina very rarely saw. "You're not my mother. I don't have to do what you say."

"Joel!" Lovina exclaimed in astonishment.

"Well, she's not."

"Sounds like someone needs a firm hand," Susan said.

"Nobody asked you!" Joel shouted. "You think you're going to move in here and be the boss of everyone, but you're not! Why don't you go home?"

Never in her life had Lovina seen him behave this way. And from the look on Susan's face, she had never been spoken to like this, either.

"Joel, *kumm mit* at once." Her tone left no room for argument. He stomped across the floor and pushed past her, then took off at a run for the kitchen door.

Lovina could not look at Daniel, who had not said more than two sentences the whole time. Despite what he'd said last night, now he must think her an awful mother. And she must apologize to Susan when at the moment, she couldn't help but agree with every word her son had said.

"I am sorry, Susan," she said stiffly. "Joel will be punished for his rudeness to you."

"I hope so," the girl said. "Daniel, will you hand me the tape? I'll finish this seam. *Der Kinner* always leave us something to clean up, don't they?"

Lovina turned and followed her boy out. But from the kitchen, she could hear Daniel's deep voice. *"Neh, denki,* I think you've done enough for the day."

Chapter 20

JOEL WAS SUITABLY DISCIPLINED, and Lovina hated every moment of having to do it. But behavior like that couldn't be allowed—Joel had not only been disrespectful to an adult, but also to Daniel and his home. To top it all off, she made her son write Susan a letter of apology, to be mailed in the morning.

"Am I done asking people for forgiveness, Mamm?" he sniffled into her shoulder as she cuddled him before bed. *"Bidde?"*

"I think so," she said softly. "But think of the peace it will bring to the ones who read your letters. And you're not alone. I had to do my share of asking forgiveness as well."

He pulled away a little to look into her face, and she gave him Daniel's handkerchief, which she had laundered but not yet given back. He blew his nose. "From who?"

"Daniel."

"For what I did?"

"*Neh,* for something that happened a long time ago, when I hurt his feelings."

"How many Communions ago? Aren't you supposed to do that right away?"

"I haven't seen him until now."

"You could have written him," her son, now the expert on asking forgiveness by letter, informed her.

"I could," she agreed. "But hurt feelings sometimes need to be made better in person. So I did it last night, and now we're *gut* friends again."

He settled down against her. In their comfortable bedroom, the lamp flickered with a golden light, and through the window, almost half of a waxing moon was rising above the pines.

"I'm glad," he said sleepily. "I like Daniel. I like it here. Can we stay?"

But she was silent for so long that he fell asleep in her arms, and she put him to bed without giving him an answer.

In the morning, she faced the truth: It was time to get serious.

"May I borrow a cell phone?" she asked Naomi after breakfast, when everyone had scattered to their chores, and Joel had set off down the lane to put his letter to Susan in the mailbox. "I would like to call my sister-in-law in Pennsylvania. Since I don't have enough money with me, I must ask her to use the business account to buy train tickets for me and Joel."

"Of course," Naomi said a little blankly. "So you are not waiting to hear from Anna Wengerd about putting Joel in school?"

"*Neh*," Lovina said. "If we can get tickets for tomorrow, he can be back in school in Willow Creek as soon as Monday."

Wordlessly, Naomi opened the cupboard and found the little phone, and after ten minutes of explanations to her sister-in-law Ruth, and a barrage of news—including that the Troyers had arrived just in time to see Barb's mother before the Lord took the latter home to Himself—she had Ruth's assurance that she would do as Lovina asked.

Half an hour later, Ruth called back to say that the tickets were bought and paid for, and seats all the way through to Lancaster reserved for the next morning. Lovina and Joel should be at the station by 4:50 a.m., half an hour before the train departed.

Tomorrow! Well, that was what she wanted, wasn't it? Honestly, she should have done this last week, Lovina thought, as she clicked off the phone. Not outstayed her welcome simply because she couldn't bring herself to drag Joel away.

No, she must be honest with herself. This horrible sinking feeling in her stomach was because she couldn't bring herself to leave Daniel. But the longer she stayed, the more difficult it would become. He had forgiven her, and they were friends again, and she must be content with that. No more daydreams about the family they could make together. Especially now that she'd seen his house and could imagine building a life in it. Of that beautiful Flying Home quilt on the bed in his front bedroom with the wonderful view.

She shut her eyes against the beauty of it, and bade it farewell.

———

"LOVINA?" Naomi asked. The young woman had gone pale. "Is everything all right?"

They were temporarily alone in the kitchen, though her girls would be in soon for mid-morning coffee.

"*Ja,*" she assured Naomi, and handed her the cell phone. "My sister-in-law has bought us tickets for tomorrow. I hope it won't be too much trouble for someone to drive us in to Libby?"

"*Neh,* any one of us can do that." Naomi watched her closely. "But ... Lovina, are you certain you want to go? And so suddenly yet?"

The young widow lifted a shoulder in a shrug. "I must. Joel must be in school, and I have a business to run. Ruth is good behind the till, but with no new stock coming in, our shelves will soon look pretty bare."

"That's not really what I meant." Naomi had done all she could to make her feel welcome—to make her want to stay. To help her see that Daniel needed time. But she couldn't very well say that out loud ... and she needed to say *something*.

"What *did* you mean?" Lovina asked. "I don't want to go, of course, because you've all been so kind. But I can only take up Adam and Zach's bedroom for so long before they will want it back." She was clearly trying to make light of a situation that upset her. "My Aendi Grace always says that both fish and family begin to smell after three days. I'm not even family and I've been here much longer than that."

Naomi felt a soft nudge in her spirit. *Speak. Now is the time.* One must always obey the promptings of the Lord, come what may.

"You may not be family now, *Liewi*. But you could be."

Lovina went still as a rabbit in a field, gazing at her wide-eyed.

"Daniel does not confide in me as much as he used to when he was a little boy," Naomi went on. "But I understand that when he was out in Whinburg Township that summer, he courted you."

"I—I— Did he tell you that?"

"In a roundabout way. Plus I had a letter the other day from Carrie Miller." The Amish grapevine. It was more reliable than any newspaper.

"Naomi, I don't want you to think that there is ... anything going on between me and Daniel under your roof." Every word came out with an effort, and Lovina's cheeks had gone scarlet.

"But you have spent a little time together."

She swallowed. "We have. But he— I mean, I—"

Naomi nodded as if Lovina had actually managed to get out one sensible word. "I hope you don't think I'm putting my hoe in your garden, where it doesn't belong. But if it makes any difference, Reuben and I, well ..." She could no longer hold back a smile of delight. "Nothing would make us happier. I just wanted you to know that."

Lovina's mouth fell open. "But the twins, they — Susan—"

Naomi's smile grew wider as she waved a hand. "That's nothing. Daniel isn't interested, and the sooner the twins figure that out, the better for their friend's feelings in the end."

Naomi had often been taken to task for being too blunt, for speaking up when silence would have been the better choice. But those who shook their heads at her did not know that many of those times had been just like this. Feeling that nudge in the spirit, and obeying it.

"I—I don't know what to say," Lovina stammered.

"Perhaps I've said too much," she admitted. "Daniel would die a thousand deaths if he knew I was being such a *Plappermaul*, but I know you won't tell on me." They both heard the sound of feet on the stairs. "You just think about it."

Lovina looked so stunned that Naomi was half afraid she'd pour the coffee into the wood stove, or put the sugar bowl in the refrigerator. She'd done the latter herself, when she'd first realized she was expecting Daniel. It was not until they were all seated at the big kitchen table that Lovina looked about her and realized the chair next to hers was still empty.

"*Wo ischt mei Joel?*" she asked. "Does it take so long to walk a quarter mile to the mailbox and back?"

"It does not," Rebecca said, her brow wrinkling in confusion. "But Lovina, no need to be frightened. We all had a big scare yesterday, and it turned out just fine. Joel isn't going to run away or be caught in a stampede or anything."

"I spoke to him very firmly about letting me know where he was," Lovina said. "If nothing else, he must obey me, whether he is safe with someone or not." She pushed away from the table, her coffee and cake forgotten. "I will just take a walk down the lane. He is probably saying *guder mariye* to every horse at the fence."

And now he would have to change that to good-bye, Naomi thought sadly.

"But Lovina—" Rebecca began.

Naomi shushed her daughter. "When you are a mother, you will understand."

"Were you like this, Mamm?" Malena asked as Lovina went out to the mud room and pulled her coat off its hook.

"Every bit, at first," Naomi said. "But not so much by the time you two came along."

"We could be halfway to the high country on the back of a runaway calf before you'd notice we were missing," Malena teased her.

"And she didn't even drop a stitch in her knitting when Joshua was born," Rebecca said, egging her sister on. "Ain't so, Mamm?"

Naomi rustled up a smile and told her, "Drink your coffee." But she gazed after Lovina as she walked rapidly down the lane and rounded the bend, and even after she was out of sight.

————

THE TWINS HAD GIVEN her a smile, anyway, Lovina thought as she walked down the lane. Maybe that had been their plan—to help her see a little humor in the situation. Ach, perhaps they were right. Deep in her heart, she knew that her need to be safe and see everyone around her safe, too, was a result of losing her parents and then

Mose. As if she could have prevented what had happened to any of them!

> But let all those that put
>   their trust in thee rejoice:
> let them ever shout for joy, be-
>   cause thou defendest them:
> let them also that love thy name
>   be joyful in thee.

The words of the fifth Psalm came to her like a whisper on the wind. With a slow nod, she acknowledged the soft sound of the Spirit. *Trust.* That was the lesson God had been trying to teach her since she'd arrived—the lesson God had prompted the twins to give just now, even if they hadn't known it.

She *had* done her best that day to keep Mose from going hunting, and he had chosen to go anyway. After that, she could do nothing but trust that God had him in His hand. Neither she nor her husband could have imagined that God would choose that trip to take Mose to Himself, just as he had taken Lovina's parents all those years ago, and even Barbara's mother this past week. Who was she to say, *No, I'm going to stop trusting You because I don't like Your timing?*

Neh, she could not. Instead, she must find the joy in trusting Him, the way a wife found joy in trusting her husband to have her best interests close to his heart. The way Joel trusted the young men here to keep him safe and teach him what he needed to know. And look—the promise of the Psalmist had come true, because in trusting the Miller men, Joel had found joy.

I like it here. Can we stay?

If only she had been able to ask that question in all the homes she had lived in during her chaotic childhood! But instead of finding joy, she had looked for safety.

Safety, she saw now, was what mere humans tried to build for themselves when what God wanted was simply for them to trust Him. And in doing that, find joy.

She was so deep in her meditations that when a boy's voice called, "Mamm!" she came to herself with a jolt, to find herself with her arms folded on the top rail of the fence and the horses rambling toward her, their kind eyes looking her over in case she was hiding a treat.

"Are you saying hello to the horses?" Joel jogged through the sere autumn grass to her side while Daniel hung back in the lane, looking as though he didn't want to interrupt.

Daniel had been with Joel for at least part of the time, just like yesterday. Why had she been so worried?

Let not your heart be troubled, the wind whispered on its way past her. *Let it not be afraid.*

"I'm sorry we took such a long time," her son went on, climbing up on the first rail and holding out a handful of grass to the horses, who looked down their noses at the dry seed heads before finally accepting them. "Daniel and I found a burrow and we wanted to see if it was a gopher or a prairie dog."

"And did you?" She smiled at Daniel, who seemed to relax visibly before he walked over to join them.

"*Neh,* we think it was abandoned," Joel said sadly. "We filled in the hole so a horse wouldn't put a foot in it."

"I see." Now was as good a moment as any to give them her news. "You were partly right just now, Joel," she said. "But I was saying good-bye to the horses, not hello. We have tickets on tomorrow morning's train from Libby to Chicago, then to Lancaster, and then Aendi Ruth and Onkel John will meet us there in an *Englisch* taxi and take us home."

"But ... tomorrow is too soon," Joel said,

looking panicked. "I was going to help Daniel some more in his house, and what about the trucks coming for the calves? Can't we stay until after Tuesday? We don't want to miss that."

Daniel hadn't said a word, but she felt his gaze like a warm hand. The hand of a friend. Despite what his mother thought, he had never said or done anything that would give her an idea that his feelings were still what they had been all those years ago, when they had been different people living different lives. Or at least, she had been living a different life. His life was here, and he had always been honest with her about that.

He would let her go with the *gut* wishes of a friend, and she would get on with the life she had chosen.

Somehow. Though it didn't hold much appeal at the moment.

"The arrangements are all made," she told Joel. "Aendi Ruth has gone to a lot of trouble and expense for us. We go tomorrow, early. We must be at the station at ten to five."

She knew Joel wanted to argue. Wanted to convince her to stay. Wanted to stop her from taking all this away from him. And yet, her boy bravely put his shoulders back, controlled the tremble in his lips, and said to Daniel with only a little huskiness in his voice, "Maybe I should help you finish that taping in the last bedroom today?"

"I'd be happy to have the help. *Denki*, Joel." He raised his gaze to meet Lovina's. "Is that all right, if he spends the day with me?"

She nodded, feeling her own throat ache. "A *gut* helper finishes what he starts."

"Do you want to come with us?" Daniel's question was gentle, but in it she understood that he was offering her the only small gift he had. To spend these last few hours together.

A gift she would be foolish to accept. She had to find the strength to get on that train tomorrow. Enjoying the day in his home, helping to bring it a few steps closer to completion, would only give her another sleepless night and more fruitless daydreams.

"*Denki,* but I must get our clothes washed and packed, and get ready for a departure I wasn't really expecting this soon."

"I wasn't expecting it, either," he confessed. "I have a hundred things to tell you, and no time to say them in."

"Come on, then, Daniel," Joel said, pulling on his jacket sleeve. "No more talking. We have to tape all those metal brackets at the top of the walls, too."

266

And Daniel allowed her son to drag him away, leaving Lovina alone with the horses and the awe-inspiring view of fields and mountains. And the nagging certainty that she was not finding the joy God wanted for her, but instead, making a terrible mistake.

Chapter 21

DANIEL HAD COME within inches of taking Lovina's hand and pulling her with him the whole way to his house. Once they got there, he would have fallen on his knees and asked her to marry him, and then together, they would walk hand in hand through the unfinished rooms and she would tell him what she wanted in them, and how they should look, and that would be the first step in the rest of their lives together.

But he hadn't.

I hope you don't think I meant anything by it. What if she rejected him again—now, when he had so much to offer her? Wasn't it better to keep his mouth shut and be satisfied with her friendship and that of her boy, rather than risk losing them both for good and ever this time?

No. That couldn't be the shape of his future—the plan of *der himmlischer Vater*, who had kept his heart free for Lovina all these years. Under his breastbone right now beat an urgency that told him he needed to speak, no matter what it cost him. To trust that God had brought her here for a reason. To push past that old fear and disappointment and risk his heart to win her. But how? When?

He did his best to push his whirling thoughts aside, and focus on teaching and working with the little boy to whom he'd have to say good-bye in the morning. The two of them put in a good day of work, and by suppertime Joel was exhausted by his labors. The boy went to bed early without complaint, and before Daniel could suggest that he and Lovina go for a walk or make up some errand out to the barn where they could talk in private, she went up to bed soon after.

Frustrated, he took himself off to the barn anyway. He didn't know what for. Maybe pounding a fist on a hay bale would help.

But there he only found the practice calf—the ragged bale of hay with a pair of horns tied to the front of it. It reminded him of how much progress Joel had made in his roping. Where would he use those skills in Whinburg Township? Roping dairy cows? What would Bishop Troyer think of that?

The workshop door closed and Daniel turned to see his brother Joshua, blinking in the lamplight. "I thought I heard someone out here," Josh said. "What's going on?"

"I—ach, I don't know." He wouldn't tell a fib, but at the same time, did his brother need to know all his business? "I thought you were finished cleaning tack."

"Days ago. I just came out to find my smokes. I left them around here somewhere." Josh looked about him as though they might scamper out from between the bales of hay.

"Don't let Dat catch you lighting up in here. All we need is for this winter feed to go up in smoke."

"I'm not stupid, Daniel." His brother eyed him. "Though I can't say the same about you."

Any other time, Daniel would have taken offense. But tonight he could hardly agree more. He plunked himself on a bale and scrubbed at his scalp.

"I've always wondered how come you never give a second look to the girls who flutter their lashes at you," Joshua went on, as though casual heart-to-heart conversations were normal between them now, the way they had been when they were children. "Now I think I know."

"Do you?" His tone was crushing.

But Joshua had never known when he was supposed to be crushed. "I don't remember how old I was when you came back from Whinburg Township, but I do remember how cranky and grouchy and hard to live with you were. Just like now."

Daniel sighed. Had he been hard to live with? It was difficult to remember anything about that dark time other than the howling disappointment and rejected love in his heart. What he did remember is being the first to ride out to the allotments to begin bringing the cattle down to the collection fields. Being alone with God in the high country had helped him to accept the fact that Lovina didn't love him enough to trust him with her future.

"If I'm so grouchy, why are you still here?"

"Because," Josh said patiently, "I have more experience with women than you do."

"Ha!" That single bark of laughter exploded from him, surprising them both. "All right, Solomon, O wise one, what would you do if a woman turned you down once and you still want to ask her a second time?"

"Women tend not to turn me down, but ... I'd ask her anyway."

Daniel just snorted. He shouldn't have said a word. He could only hope that someday the woman would come along who would knock all this cockiness and worldly self-assurance out of his youngest brother.

"What's the worst that could happen?" Joshua stomped in where an angel with any brains at all would fear to tread. "She says no, and then she gets on the train and you never see her again. Win-win."

Daniel got up to leave.

"But let's pretend for a minute that she says yes. Or even maybe. She goes home because she has to, and all she does is remember how much she misses you. Maybe she's as grouchy as you are, and poor Joel begs to be shipped back out west with a tag on his jacket addressed to the Circle M. The bottom line is, she comes back here on purpose this time and you live happily ever after."

There was no response a man could make to this except an incredulous glare.

"Trust me, Daniel," Josh said. "This is the plot from a classic *Englisch* movie."

Between clenched teeth, Daniel said, "I've never seen an *Englisch* movie."

"Well, you're missing out. At the very end, the guy always has to open his mouth and say something, because the girl is never going to."

"Ain't so?" He managed some sarcasm this time. "Is this some kind of law in *Englisch* movies?"

"*Neh*, but you know as well as I do it might as well be a law with us. No Amish girl is going to be that forward and ask you first."

"You'd be surprised," he said, thinking of Susan Bontrager eyeballing his windows. He knew perfectly well she'd been silently estimating how much blue fabric she would need to cover them.

"Yeah, maybe," Joshua conceded. "I've heard the twins talking about some pretty complicated maneuvers just to get a man's attention. It's scary. Anyway. Lovina's had some experiences the rest of us haven't, but the bottom line is, she's Amish and she's not going to speak up. You've got to do it or you'll just be moping around the ranch for the next ten years. None of us can stand that. Trust me. Oh, hey, there are my smokes."

Joshua swiped them off one of the crossbeams and went out by the big sliding doors, whistling with the cheerfulness of a man who has done his good deed for the year and could now go carouse with his worldly friends with a clear conscience.

Daniel sank down once more on the hay bale and gazed gloomily at the horns of the practice calf. The Lovina he had known that summer had worn her heart on her sleeve. Every emotion had been written right there in her face, much as she had tried to hide it from anyone but him. But Josh was right—the Lovina of today had learned in a hard school to keep her thoughts and feelings to herself. Only with Joel did Daniel see glimmers of the girl she had been.

She had asked Daniel's forgiveness. He must not forget that. Surely it hadn't just been so she could get on the train and, like Joshua, go on her way rejoicing that she'd done the right thing? And her insistence on telling him the roots of her need for safety—was that so he would understand why she had sent him away? But now that she was a woman grown, with her own choices to make and her hand firmly in that of a God she trusted to protect her, would she answer his question differently?

There was only one way to find out, and he was running out of time.

————

JOEL DIDN'T WANT to wake up at three-thirty, if the complaints coming from behind his and Lovina's closed bedroom door were any indication. But as Daniel padded down the stairs to poke up the wood stove, he heard Lovina's soft voice and the thump of feet on the floor as the boy gave in to the inevitable. Smiling, he found Dat in the kitchen and Mamm already at the propane range.

"I made the cinnamon rolls last night so I could bake them first thing," she said. "Joel might like one or two for a snack along about mid-morning."

"We'll make sandwiches for their lunch," Malena said as she came in with Rebecca, yawning wide enough to fit a whole cinnamon roll. "Is that coffee ready?"

With the rolls in the oven, Mamm got busy with frying pan and bacon, and soon the kitchen was a joyful noise of activity.

Snug in his coat, the black stocking cap Mamm had knitted him for Christmas last year pulled down to keep his ears warm, Daniel took a cup of coffee with him out to the barn. Frost glittered in the lamplight, every surface rimed with it and the puddles in the wagon ruts frozen over. The October sun might keep winter at bay during the daytime, but the night knew that November—and the Montana winter—was right around the corner.

He fed Cody, their other buggy horse, and then hitched him up so that he would be ready inside the doors when they came out after breakfast. Back in the kitchen, it seemed that the more he tried to hold on to each minute, each expression in Lovina's eyes, each smile, the giggle that finally came out of Joel at Adam and Zach's teasing, the faster the time slipped away. Half an hour later he was swinging Lovina's and Joel's little suitcases into the back of the buggy and turning on the driving lamps. Lovina climbed into the passenger side after Joel, who sat in the middle where it was warm under the buggy blanket, and the minutes on the Circle M ran out.

Daniel clicked his tongue to Cody and they set off down the lane, ice crunching under the buggy's wheels.

The county highway was deserted at this time of the morning, and when they rolled through it, so was Mountain Home. But Joel didn't see any of it—he had fallen asleep again, leaning against Lovina's side within the circle of her right arm. Every time Daniel moved, their arms brushed, sending a tingle up Daniel's side.

He could be nineteen again, and she a year younger, and it felt exactly the same as when they were courting.

Mountain Home was receding behind them now. He had only five miles left.

"Lovina," he began hoarsely, "I hope you will have a safe journey."

Why had he said that? He hadn't meant to. What was the matter with him?

"*Denki*, Daniel," she said. "I hope so, too. It is very kind of you to take us."

"It was not kind—it was necessary." Then he plunged in. "I wish I didn't have to take you at all."

"Oh." With a muffled gasp, she ducked her head. "Well. I—I suppose one of the other boys might have, then. I'm sorry—I know you're busy."

What was she talking about? Then he could have slapped himself for an utter fool. "*Neh*, that's not what I meant. I meant that I wish you didn't have to go. At all."

Had any three sentences ever been so hard to get out?

"But I do," she said sadly. "We were never supposed to be here. It has been wonderful *gut*, getting to know your family, and becoming friends again. But I suppose like all *gut* things, even this has to come to an end."

"Is that what you want?" he asked desperately.

"I don't have a choice. Joel must be in school, and I have a home and a business to run."

"Didn't you say that your sister-in-law was good at running the business?"

"She is very good at the cash register, and keeping track of the accounts. I have no doubt that she will have corrected every error in the ledger that I've made since Mose died, and the books will be so painfully up to date that there will be nothing left for me to do."

"Then you should let her do that."

"Ruth can't help it," she said with a laugh, careful not to disturb Joel.

Three miles left. He must turn the conversation.

"But there is more to an antique shop than the ledgers," she said before he could. "We all have our gifts, and I had begun to think that one of mine must be to take something like a dining table and four mismatched chairs, give it a little elbow grease, and set it."

"Set it?"

"Yes—I make displays with the inventory. Not whole rooms, but enough for people to see what could be, in their own homes. I take some quilted place mats, and some china we found at an estate sale, and someone's grandmother's old silver, buffed up for the occasion. In the middle I might put a Depression glass bowl and two candlesticks. People don't want to just buy old stuff. They want to buy an atmosphere for their homes. A future. A vision."

"And you make them think your antiques can give them this new future."

"That's the idea."

Two miles.

"Would you do that in my home?"

She glanced at him curiously. "I don't know how well my antiques would look in your beautiful log house, Daniel. You want things that look like they belong, the way your parents' furniture is so comfortable and welcoming."

"I didn't mean that. I meant ... if you stayed. And became my wife. And made my house a home. With me."

Her mouth dropped open and for a moment he had to look away. Not because Cody was in any danger of going off the road, but because the sheer shock in her face made him realize that never in a thousand years should he have said those awkward words.

If only he could relive the last ten seconds! He thought he might just die of humiliation.

"Daniel, I—I—"

"It's all right," he said on a long, hopeless breath. "Forget I said anything."

"Do you—you mean you still—"

"It's all right," he said again, when it wasn't all right, and never would be for as long as he lived.

Now they were in Libby, the streets alive with hunters getting an early start, and there was the train station. There was nothing to do but turn in and guide Cody over to the rail.

"But do you?" she said fiercely. "Care?"

"I do," he said. Might as well say it, and have done. "I always have."

The bright lights in the parking lot woke Joel and he stretched, pulling the buggy blanket off them so that the cold pounced on their legs like a cat. In the distance, Daniel heard the whistle of the Amtrak train at the crossing away up the valley. The whistle that usually woke him and Dat both, and got their day started.

"Train's early," he said. "We'd better get moving."

"Daniel Miller! Is that all you're going to say?"

she demanded incredulously. "You drop something like that on me and then tell me the train's early?"

But he was already out of the buggy and looping Cody's rein over the bar. With a suitcase in each hand, he led the way through the station, Lovina sputtering like a tea kettle as she gripped Joel's hand and practically had to jog to keep up.

Why was he acting like this? Like she had already said good-bye and the matter was closed? He felt as though he was watching some other poor fool make an idiot of himself.

The station was a bare-bones affair, with no luggage service, no telephones, no vending machines. Only a ticket taker and a platform and a train arriving with a roar and a scream of brakes.

"It'll only stop for a minute." He found their car and heaved the suitcases up, then boosted Joel up the high steps after them.

"Stop being so high-handed for two seconds!" Lovina exclaimed.

The train whistled and she jumped for the door, scrambling up the steps.

Gripping the sides of the door so it wouldn't close, she turned. "What if I wanted to?" she cried.

"Wanted to what?" The train jerked, and the door began to close automatically.

"Put a bunch of antiques in your log house?"

"If you were there, you could put anything you wanted in it, and I'd be happy."

The door closed in her face, and through its window he could see her bang on it in frustration. Then as the train picked up speed, he thought he saw her say something.

Was she saying *yes*? Blast it, he couldn't see!

With a shriek of its whistle that deafened him and probably poor Cody too, on the other side of the building, the train left the station and took away the two people he loved most in the whole world.

Chapter 22

"HE IS GOING to mess this up." Joshua felt the certainty of it down to his bones before the rattle of the buggy had even faded.

The family had gathered on the verandah to wave good-bye, for all the good it had done. The pair in the buggy were too bogged down in their own pasts to even see them, never mind return a wave.

Dat merely grunted and told Adam and Zach to come with him to do the chores. He told Joshua, too, but he had bigger fish to fry.

"What do you mean, Josh?" Malena wanted to know, hurrying back into the warmth of the kitchen. "Mess what up?"

He shook his head at his sister. "Are you so blind? Daniel's crazy in love with that girl, and he hasn't got a clue how to tell her."

"He is not!" Rebecca slammed the kitchen door and stomped over to the wood stove to warm up. "You're the one who's blind. Why can't anyone but Malena and me see that Susan Bontrager is the perfect wife for him? She's our friend, and we already love her."

"*And* she's in love with him," Malena added.

"*And* he doesn't care," Josh mimicked her, shaking his head in pity at their continuing delusions. "He told me himself it's Lovina, no one else. And now look." He waved a hand in the direction of the road. "He's going to put her on that train and spend the next decade making us miserable because he doesn't have the guts to speak up."

"Don't talk about your brother that way," Mamm said severely. "Or I'll give Rebecca the morning off and make you do all these dishes."

"Keep talking, Josh," Rebecca said with a sweet smile.

"I told him last night exactly what he's supposed to do. But will he do it?" Josh tipped his head back in an appeal to the universe. "No."

"All right, Mr. Smarty Pants, I'll bite." Malena began to clear the breakfast dishes. "What, in your oh-so-experienced opinion, is he supposed to do?"

She had no idea about his experience. "In every *Englisch* romance movie ever made, the guy chases the girl to the airport or the train and proposes," Josh informed her. "So that's what I told him. And you know what he said?"

"Mind your own business?" Rebecca inquired of the sink.

"I've never seen an Englisch movie," Josh said in a passable imitation of his brother's bass voice. "Like *that* was the point, the big galoot!"

"There will be no talk of worldly things like movies in my kitchen," Mamm said severely. "And instead of criticizing your brother behind his back, you should either help him or help your sister with the dishes. Your choice."

"Like Joshua would ever help anybody with anything."

Josh eyed Malena, absorbing the sting of her careless words the way the water in a pond closed around a rock. If anyone cared to look, they'd see a lot of rocks down there at the bottom. "What's that supposed to mean?"

"Never mind, you two," Rebecca told them. "Mamm, what did *you* mean?"

But their mother only shrugged as though she

had the weight of the world on her shoulders. "I don't know. But I wish there was something."

Joshua stared at her. There *was* something. "Mamm, how fast can you pack a bag with Daniel's stuff? Maybe two weeks' worth?"

Her gaze held his. "Five minutes. But getting to the station is the hard part. Your father will never let you take one of the cutting horses, and the pickup wagon will be too slow."

He shook his head. "Pack that bag. I'll be right back."

He jogged across the still dark yard to the tack room, which he had begun to think of as his domain since Dat made him do so much work out there. So he'd made a little stash of life's necessities. He opened an old saddlebag and rifled past the disguise of litter on top to where he kept his smokes, some money, a street map of Seattle for when he got there someday, and his phone.

Tyler Carson, who slept in his parents' basement and could count on some privacy, answered on the first ring. "Yo."

"I need the car. Can you pick me up?"

"Dude, what time is it? I was asleep."

"It's an emergency. I have to get to Libby before the train leaves."

"Dude," Tyler said plaintively, but Josh could already hear him rustling around, then the clank of his belt buckle being dragged across the floor.

"Thanks, man. Meet you out on the road."

When he let himself back into the kitchen, Mamm was ready with a gym bag, a plastic container full of food, and a mystified expression. "How are you—" she began.

He took both bag and container and gave her a kiss. That startled her so much she forgot to ask any more questions, just stood there with her mouth open while he did a dance step around Malena and Rebecca and out the door.

He jogged the quarter mile to the road, turned right, and slung the gym bag over his shoulder while he kept up an easy pace. One thing about ranch work—it kept him in shape. Before long he heard the Dart's engine, and when it pulled up beside him he slid in. "My man," he said with satisfaction as Ty wound the thing up and made the seven or so miles to Libby in five minutes flat.

The train's whistle screamed as Josh jumped out and ran for the platform.

But instead of three happy people hugging, or three happy people on the train disappearing into the distance, there was only Daniel, standing there empty-handed and looking as though he'd just been hit by a brick and hadn't fallen yet.

Daniel looked up as Josh grabbed his arm. In the too-bright platform lights, his brother's eyes were a pair of black holes filled with … Josh couldn't tell what.

"Did you ask her?" he demanded.

Daniel didn't even seem surprised that he was there. "Yes."

"And she got on the train anyway?" Here was a plot development he'd never seen coming. "Are you kidding me? She said no?"

"I don't know. I don't think so. But I don't know."

Josh felt like taking him by the shoulders and giving him a good shake. Instead, he thrust the lunch container into his hands and shrugged the bag's strap off his shoulders to drop it over his brother's head. "Come on."

"Where?" Daniel looked down at the bag as if he didn't know what it was for.

"I'll tell you on the way."

The poor guy was so demoralized that he actually obeyed, following Josh out into the parking lot to the car.

"Ty, out," Josh ordered. "I'm taking Daniel to Whitefish."

"Dude! What am I supposed to do?"

Good gravy, couldn't anybody think for himself around here? "Take the buggy to your place. Tie the horse where he can graze. I'll be back before lunch."

"But I don't know how to drive a buggy!"

"That's okay, Cody knows his way back. Watch out for hunters."

And with that, he shoved the Dart into gear and laid rubber out of the parking lot. Tyler might not be the brightest bulb in the box, but he was good about keeping the car in shape and its tank full. That was their deal, and so far he'd stood by it. What they were going to do when Josh went to Seattle, he wasn't sure. Maybe Ty would go with him.

But first he had to solve his brother's problem.

It was a little less than two hours to Whitefish by road, but the train would have to go north in a route shaped like an upside-down U. Josh would cut across the two ends of the U and arrive at roughly the same time the train did.

He made it to the Amtrak station at Whitefish with minutes to spare.

It was a good thing that deep down, he loved his brother. Because man, the twists and turns in that road had been hairy. Daniel, for once, had been scared spitless—and silent—first because he hadn't known that Josh had a driver's license, and second because the road was a big old grizzly *bear* of a road.

"I didn't risk both our lives and my investment in this car for you to mess up twice in one morning," he told Daniel sternly as he pulled up at the curb in front of the depot building—just as fake German looking as the one in Libby, why was that? Daniel got out and slammed the door shut, but for some reason, it seemed he thought Josh would be getting out and going up those steps with him. Just in case, Josh leaned over and smacked the door lock down.

"I can't go to Pennsylvania," Daniel said stubbornly, bending to speak through the cracked window. "There's too much work to do at home."

The whistle shrieked as the train pulled in and slid to a stop, its length stretching away down the railyard behind the parking lot.

"Train's here. You're going. Go buy a ticket. End of story."

"This isn't a story!" Daniel shouted at him. "Now open this door!"

"Nope. Good luck."

And Josh spun the wheel and squealed out of

the parking lot, leaving his brother standing open-mouthed on the pavement.

———

ONLY TWO THINGS had kept Lovina from completely losing control of herself over the past two hours. Joel, of course, and having to get him to their seats and settled in while answering a hundred questions. The second thing was the grandeur of God's creation as the sun rose to illuminate it in all its glory. Half of her took in the splendid views of mountain peaks and swaths of gleaming snow mixed with the dark green of the pines, and let them sink into her soul. The other half listened to Joel grouse about having to go back to school instead of being where he was needed and wanted to be. And under it all she heard Daniel's voice, like an echo that would not fade. Every word pulled, agonizingly, from the deepest place within him.

If you stayed. And became my wife. And made my house a home. With me.

And what had she done? She'd been all in a flurry trying to get on the stupid train. Her mind stuck on how expensive the tickets had been. She should have thrown all that to the winds and flung herself into his arms, shouting "Yes!" to the heavens, and let it go to Chicago without her.

Had any woman ever been so hopeless? Now he probably thought she had rejected him again, because saying yes to a closed window as the train slid away from him was about as useful as teats on a bull.

She was a fool. But she had made a choice, and there was nothing left to do now but get on with the consequences.

"Mamm, I have to go to the bathroom."

"You know where it is. At the end of the car. Be back in five minutes, though. Our stop here is only ten minutes and I don't want you in the way of people getting on."

But he was not back in five minutes. Anxiously, she clutched her handbag crossways across her body as she stood in the aisle, searching the car for him. Around her, the newcomers settled into their seats with a great fuss of getting suitcases into racks and settling coffee into cup holders. But no Joel.

According to her watch on its modest leather band, eight minutes had passed. What was he doing?

And then the bottom fell out of her world as simultaneously, the train whistle blew, the announcement came overhead that they would be departing shortly, and a small Amish boy in a black wool coat and black hat dashed across the platform and into the depot, disappearing into a crowd of strangers that swallowed him up in the space of a heartbeat.

"Joel!" she shrieked, and a dozen people stared at her. What was he doing? Was he running for safety?

She had only seconds.

She snatched up their bags, one in each hand, and pushed down the aisle like a battering ram, head down and apologizing for the irritation in her wake. She fell out the door of the train and on to the concrete platform, landing half on her knees and half on Joel's little soft-sider. The train shrieked and pulled away, but she was already running for the depot door.

Every Amish mother had heard terrible tales of children being snatched. From roadside produce stands, from crowded towns—even, in Whinburg Township, from an orchard. Two girls had been taken, their brother only a few feet away.

Heart pounding, she whirled from one side to the other, trying to see her boy among the people in the depot. People rolling bags back and forth, hunters claiming rifles at the checked baggage, Amtrak employees rushing hither and yon on business of their own—where was her son? This was her worst nightmare come true. Joel in danger and not one soul for hundreds of miles who cared or could help her.

Mei Gott, hilfe mich! The cry went up from her soul. *Help me find him—let him be safe!*

And then—and then—she saw a familiar pair of broad shoulders. A black hat. That long stride, those capable hands ... and holding one of those hands was Joel.

Lovina's knees went out from under her and she sat abruptly on one of their bags, as the relief and gratitude for her loving Father rolled up through her body like a shout. She burst into such a storm of tears she thought her ribs might crack.

"Lovina-love—"

"Mamm, Mamm, it's all right."

"Are you hurt, *Liewi?*"

"Mamm, you're scaring me."

She pulled her boy into her arms, and somehow Daniel's arms were around both of them, and she could not stop—couldn't—stop—hugging him. Saying the words that came out of her as though a dam had broken.

"I love you—I love you—never leave me again."

"I won't, Mamm. But I saw Daniel in the station and—"

"Yes," she gasped, and lifted her face to search Daniel's, that beloved face that had haunted her dreams for a decade. "Yes, I will marry you and love you and make your home and put antiques in it that you will hate and—"

A smile spread across his face and lit his eyes with joy. "I told you this morning—as long as you are there, *Liewi*, you may put anything in our house you like."

"Our house?" Joel looked from one to the other. "Whose house?"

"Our house on the Circle M," Daniel said softly. "Our house that God will fill with love and joy, just as soon as your *mamm* and I are married."

"You're getting married?" Joel said in disbelief. "We're staying on the ranch?"

"*Ja*, Joel." Lovina let Daniel pull her to her feet. "We have a lot of work to do to finish up our lives in Pennsylvania, but in the end we'll come back and stay."

"Hey, there's Joshua, coming in the door!" Joel ran to him. "Josh, guess what! The train left without us and Mamm and Daniel are getting married!"

Lovina stared from one Miller brother to the other. "I don't understand. What are you doing here?"

Joshua hefted their sadly squashed suitcases. "Car's right outside. I had a feeling I should stick around for half an hour and make sure my brother finally got his happy ending."

Joel ran after him through the doors to the parking lot. Following more slowly, Daniel pulled her against his side.

"Are you going to tell me what is going on?" she asked him. "Other than the *gut Gott* making a miracle just for us?"

"Let's just say that Joshua is full of surprises and more than a few secrets," he said softly. "But he has also changed everything."

"Maybe that was part of the miracle."

The double doors closed behind them and for a brief moment, the roar of the depot was silenced and above the sound of Joel's chatter with Joshua, the two of them heard a strange, wild sound in the sky.

Canada geese. Skeins of them, in ragged *V* formations, heading south.

"Flying home," Lovina said on a long breath.

"Just like us," Daniel said. He took her in his arms and lowered his mouth to hers. Claiming her, as she claimed him. Completely. Whole-heartedly.

Now, and for always.

Epilogue

WHERE ON EARTH could they be?

Naomi Miller paced the kitchen, but every time she looked at the clock beside the back door, its hands had barely moved. Maybe the batteries were dying. She marched into the living room to look at the clock in the china cabinet in the *Eck*. The clock had been her engagement gift from Reuben and was the pretty kind with revolving balls under a glass dome. But it showed the same time.

Seven thirty.

And then eight o'clock.

And finally, after a century in which a glacier or two probably melted in the national park, eight thirty.

Something had gone wrong. Daniel would never do this. Something had happened to him. Her breakfast did a somersault in her stomach, and she bolted for the bathroom, where she threw up whatever had been left undigested.

"Mamm, what's the matter?" Rebecca called down. Both Malena and Rebecca were supposed to be sweeping the upper floor and scrubbing the bathroom. "We can hear you pacing from up here."

She rinsed her mouth with a little toothpaste while the toilet flushed, and joined her daughters in the kitchen. "Daniel and Joshua aren't back yet," she said tersely. "I'm worried."

Both their gazes went to the clock. "Ach," Rebecca murmured. "That is strange. I didn't realize it was so late."

"Are you sure they're not here?" Malena went to the window overlooking the yard.

"Sure and certain. That buggy hasn't come home yet. I'm also sure that it doesn't take four hours to drive to Libby and back."

"Well, the odds of Joshua coming home at all were never great," Rebecca pointed out. "Did Daniel have errands he meant to do in town?"

"If he did, he won't find anything open except gas stations and the fishing and hunting supply,"

Malena told her twin. "And it's not likely he'd go in *there* during opening week. Too crowded."

"Should I get Dat?" Rebecca asked. Anxiety had begun to bloom in her eyes. "He could take the pickup wagon and look."

"We won't bother your father when the trucks are coming for the cattle on Tuesday. He and your brothers have enough to do, making sure those calves are healthy and fit to travel. Get your coats, *Dochsdere*. We'll go ourselves."

Malena headed for the stairs. Halfway up, she turned. "If we find him, and everything is all right, can we stop at the quilt shop? It will be open by the time we come back through Mountain Home."

"How can you think of quilts when your brother may have been run over by a hunter in a four-by-four?" came Rebecca's voice from the upstairs hall. "Come *on*, Malena."

In her own room, Naomi took her black away bonnet from the shelf in the closet, and located her scarf and leather gloves in the bottom drawer of the dresser. Her stomach still hadn't settled, and she laid a hand on her middle as though that might calm it.

And she reached for the one thing that would calm her heart.

Dear Lord, please keep my boys safe. Please wrap Your loving hand around both of them in protection and care. Help me to put my trust in You, and take this fear from me. Be with us on this little trip today, and if it be Thy will, help me find Daniel and Joshua safe and sound. In Jesus' name I pray, amen.

Out in the kitchen, she scribbled a note for Reuben. She could call him, of course, but he and the boys would see them driving down the lane, so there didn't seem much point in using up the balance on the phone card for that. However, she would be smart to take the phone with her. At least she'd remembered that much—half the time she forgot it was in the cupboard. She slipped it into her handbag, put on her coat, and went out to harness Hester.

Ten minutes later, they were on their way down the lane. Out in the field, Reuben looked up. She had the window open, and gave him what she hoped was a reassuring wave, and he lifted his hand in return—slowly, as if he were trying to figure out why she hadn't told him she would need the pickup buggy today. With its open back, he used it to transport big things like hay bales and fertilizer. When she and the girls went to town, they tended to use the closed family buggy or the "courting" buggy that no one seemed to be using for much courting.

Ach, when she got back, she would tell her husband she'd been worried. And he would tell her she was a silly thing, and kiss her worries away. But by then, Daniel and Joshua would both be home, and she would laugh and make an extra special dinner to make up for not being there to make lunch.

Already the morning was half gone.

"Keep your eyes open," Rebecca said over Hester's rapid clip-clop along the county highway.

As if anyone needed to tell Naomi that. With three of them crammed together on the only bench, there were nothing but eyes looking from side to side, examining every lane and wagon. When they came to the outskirts of Mountain Home, though, it got more difficult. It was Saturday, and one of the *Englisch* long weekends, and there were hunters and families and vehicles everywhere she looked.

How was she going to see her boys in all this traffic?

"Mamm!" Malena cried. "Look, in the driveway of that gray house. That's Cody and our buggy!"

Naomi's eyes nearly fell out of her head. They

were sitting at one of Mountain Home's two stop signs, and when she flicked on the turn signal for a left turn, the truck with Washington plates behind her honked his horn at the delay. Hester flinched, but she didn't bolt. Naomi must be calm for the horse's sake, and for her daughters' sake, too.

"Ignore him," she said between her teeth, half to herself and half to the horse, and guided Hester into the turn.

She pulled into the driveway of the gray house, mystified, and brought Hester to a stop next to their other horse. Cody looked up and nickered in recognition, as close as a horse could get to "boy, am I glad to see you." He had eaten a circle of grass around himself, as far as the rein looped around the power pole would allow.

"Poor thing, he's been here for ages," Malena said. "That's not like Daniel. Come on, we'd better ask at the house."

The three of them climbed the steps and Malena knocked briskly.

No one answered, but the air seemed to be vibrating just a little. So were the planks of the porch. "Someone's playing music downstairs," Rebecca said. "They can't hear us. Try again."

Malena pounded on the door with her fist and

rang the bell repeatedly for good measure. The music shut off and after an excruciating wait, the door opened.

"Help you?" The young man looked them over owlishly, as if they'd awakened him from a sound sleep. How could anyone sleep in all that racket?

"Hello," Naomi said. "I'm Naomi Miller—Daniel and Joshua's mother. Are they here?"

"Seriously?" Sheer relief washed over his face, which was not the reaction she'd been expecting. "Dude—I mean, ma'am, Josh said he'd be back by now but that horse eats way more than I thought. Is it okay that he's tied up there? I didn't want to let him loose or anything in case he got away."

"*Ja*—I mean, yes, he's fine there. But what did you mean, back by now? Do you know where they are?"

The young man scrubbed his scalp with one hand, and his hair stood up in clumps on that side of his head. "I know where he was going. Dude—ma'am—Josh ditched me. Went to Whitefish and told me to bring the buggy back here. I never drove a buggy in my life. It was nuts."

"Whitefish," Rebecca repeated. She tilted her head in her away bonnet as if that would help her hear better. "Why? What's in Whitefish?"

"I dunno. The train, I guess."

Naomi struggled to make sense of this. It was like trying to cook with a recipe that had holes in it, and having to guess what might have been there. "So that's where Joshua is. Do you happen to know where Daniel is? Joshua's older brother? He was the one who was supposed to be in the buggy."

Please let him be all right. Please let there be a logical explanation.

"I guess he went with Josh. Dude turfed me out of the car and took off with him in the front seat."

"To Whitefish," Rebecca said again, as though to make sure.

"For goodness sake, Whitefish or Wyoming, it's all impossible," Naomi blurted in exasperation. "Joshua doesn't know how to drive a car!"

"He does so," the young man said, blinking at her. "Got his license in the spring and went in with me on a totally sick Dodge Dart."

There was nothing about this revelation that made the least bit of sense to Naomi. This disheveled boy was speaking words that might be *Englisch*, but they had no meaning.

"So let me get this right," Rebecca said, holding up a hand. "Our youngest brother took our eldest brother to Whitefish. In a car. That he is part owner of. With you."

"No, he owns it. I insure it. Maintain it, stuff like that. Works out about even. But hey—that's a gnarly road. Though if anything can make it, the Dart can."

Rebecca snapped her fingers. "Obviously something happened with Lovina and Joel. They took the car to try to beat the train to its next stop. Whitefish."

"But did they, is the question," Malena said, nodding. "I guess we'll find out. How long does it take to drive back from there if you're not trying to beat a train?"

But this was too much arithmetic for the young man.

It was too much of everything for Naomi.

Joshua was driving a car.

Oh, this would break Reuben's heart.

Her stomach heaved and she made it to the porch railing just in time.

THE END

A note from Adina

I hope you've enjoyed this first book about the Miller family on the Circle M. If you subscribe to my newsletter, you'll hear about new releases in the series, my research in Montana, and snippets about quilting and writing and chickens—my favorite subjects!

Visit www.adinasenft.com to sign up, and be sure to browse my other Amish novels set in beautiful Whinburg Township, Pennsylvania.

Want to know what happens to the Montana Millers in book two? Turn the page for a little hint!

Sneak peek
THE AMISH COWBOY'S BABY

A lonely prodigal, a cowboy rebel, a secret baby. A recipe for disaster ... or for unexpected love?

Joshua Miller is the youngest in the Miller family —and the one most likely to break his mother's heart. The minute he can sneak away, he's out with his *Englisch* friends, planning when he'll jump the fence. It's all good times and bad choices ... until the day he finds a baby at the door with a note pinned to the blanket saying the child is his.

Sara Fischer once thought the grass was greener on the other side, only to discover that coming back to the church can be harder than leaving it. Now she's returned to Montana ranch country, where the only job she can find is on the

Circle M—as a nanny. She may not be very good with babies, but she knows a hurting man when she sees one—and she responds to Joshua in a way she never has with anyone else.

The Amish way of life is the fence that divides them. But can a baby's trusting smile be the key that opens their hearts to each other—and to God?

Look for *The Amish Cowboy's Baby* at your favorite retailer!

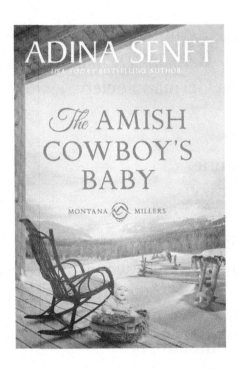

Glossary

Spelling and definitions from Eugene S. Stine, *Pennsylvania German Dictionary* (Birdboro, PA: Pennsylvania German Society, 1996).

Words used:
Aendi: auntie
batzich: crazy
bidde: please
Boppli, Bopplin: baby, babies
Bob: bun; hairstyle worn by Amish girls and women
Bruder: brother
Daadi: Grandfather
demut: humble
denki, denkes: thank you, thanks

Dochsder, Dochsdere: daughter, daughters

Dokterfraa: female herbal healer

Duchly: headscarf

dei Fraa: your wife

der Herr: the Lord

der Himmlischer Vater: the heavenly Father

Englisch: non Amish people, also their language

Gmee: The church, the local Amish congregation

Gott: God

guder mariye: good morning

guder owed: good afternoon

guder nacht: good night

gut: good

ja: yes

Ja, ich komme: Yes, I'm coming

Kapp: prayer covering worn by plain women

Kinner: children

Kumm hier: Come here

Kumme mit: Come with me

Liewi: dear, darling

Loblied: The traditional second hymn sung in the Amish service

Maedel: maiden, young girl

Maud: maid, household helper

Mamm: Mom, Mother

Mammi: Grandmother

Mei Gott, hilfe mich! My God, help me!

mei Hatz: my heart

mei Sohn: my son

neh: no

nix: short for *nichts,* meaning, *is it not* or *ain't so?*

Ordnung: discipline, or standard of behavior and dress unique to each community

Rumspringe: "running around"—the season of freedom for Amish youth between sixteen and the time they marry or join church

Schweschder: sister

Uffgeva: giving up of one's will, submission

verhuddelt: confused, mixed-up

Was ischt? What is it?

Wie geht's? How goes it?

Wo ischt mei Joel? Where is my Joel?

Youngie: Amish young people 16 years and older

Also by Adina Senft

The Whinburg Township Amish series

The Wounded Heart

The Hidden Life

The Tempted Soul

Herb of Grace

Keys of Heaven

Balm of Gilead

The Longest Road

The Highest Mountain

The Sweetest Song

"The Heart's Return" (novella)

The Montana Millers series

The Amish Cowboy

The Amish Cowboy's Baby

The Amish Cowboy's Bride

The Amish Cowboy's Letter

The Amish Cowboy's Makeover

The Amish Cowboy's Home

The Smoke River series

Grounds to Believe

Pocketful of Pearls

The Sound of Your Voice

Over Her Head

———

The Glory Prep series (faith-based young adult)

Glory Prep

The Fruit of My Lipstick

Be Strong and Curvaceous

Who Made You a Princess?

Tidings of Great Boys

The Chic Shall Inherit the Earth

About the Author

USA Today bestselling author Adina Senft grew up in a plain house church, where she was often asked by outsiders if she was Amish (the answer was no).

She holds a PhD in Creative Writing from Lancaster University in the UK. Adina was the winner of RWA's RITA Award for Best Inspirational Novel in 2005, a finalist for that award in 2006, and was a Christy Award finalist in 2009. She appeared in the 2016 documentary film *Love Between the Covers*, is a popular speaker and convention panelist, and has been a guest on many podcasts, including Worldshapers and Realm of Books.

She writes steampunk adventure and mystery as Shelley Adina; and as Charlotte Henry, writes classic Regency romance. When she's not writing, Adina is usually quilting, sewing historical costumes, or enjoying the garden with her flock of rescued chickens.

Adina loves to talk with readers about books, quilting, and chickens!
www.adinasenft.com
adinasenft@comcast.net

Made in the USA
Las Vegas, NV
17 December 2023

82996845R00194